REVOLUTION
Is Not a Dinner Party

Ying Chang Compestine

YING CHANG COMPESTINE

REVOLUTION
Is Not a Dinner Party

A NOVEL

SQUARE
FISH

HENRY HOLT AND COMPANY ✤ NEW YORK

In memory of Dr. Chang Sin Liu—
I love you, Daddy!

SQUARE
FISH

An Imprint of Macmillan

REVOLUTION IS NOT A DINNER PARTY. Copyright © 2007 by Ying
Chang Compestine. Map copyright © 2007 by Jennifer Thermes. All rights reserved.
Printed in the United States of America by LSC Communications,
Harrisonburg, Virginia. For information, address Square Fish,
175 Fifth Avenue, New York, NY 10010.

Square Fish and the Square Fish logo are trademarks of Macmillan and are used by
Henry Holt and Company under license from Macmillan.

Library of Congress Cataloging-in-Publication Data
Compestine, Ying Chang.
Revolution is not a dinner party / Ying Chang Compestine.
p.   cm.
Summary: Starting in 1972 when she is nine years old, Ling, the daughter of two doctors,
struggles to make sense of the communists' Cultural Revolution, which empties stores of
food, homes of appliances deemed "bourgeois," and people of laughter.
ISBN 978-0-312-58149-7
[1. China—History—Cultural Revolution, 1966–1976—Juvenile fiction.
2. China—History—Cultural Revolution, 1966–1976—Fiction.
3. Persecution—Fiction.   4. Family life—China—Fiction.   5. Physicians—Fiction.
6. Communism—Fiction.]   I. Title.
PZ7.C73615Rev 2007   [Fic]—dc22   2006035465

Originally published in the United States by Henry Holt and Company
Square Fish logo designed by Filomena Tuosto
Design by Meredith Pratt
First Square Fish Edition: September 2009
15 17 19 20 18 16
mackids.com
AR: 4.7 / F&P: W / LEXILE: 740L

Contents

1 LITTLE FLOWER

Father's Ponytails   5
Waste Is a Great Crime   18
Bartering with Comrade Li   25
Homemade Ice Cream and German Chocolate   36
"Bloodsucking Landlord!"   52
Will Butterflies Land on Me?   66
The Terrifying Birthday   76
Crushed under the Heel   90

2 BAMBOO IN THE WIND

Revolution Is Not a Dinner Party   103
Drawing a Class Line   115
Dark Clouds   125
Would I Ever See Him Again?   137
The Long White Rope   151
Shopping with Mother   161

3 BRIDGE BEHIND MAO

Angry Tiger   175
Too Proud to Bend   183
Waiting for Daddy   191
Howling Wolf   207
Pig Fat   220
Golden Gate Bridge   230

AUTHOR'S NOTE   245

HISTORICAL BACKGROUND   247

To Pastry Shop

ZHONGSHAN AVENUE

Milk Tree
Flower

Home
(staff apartments)

#4 City Hospital

Victory Road

Flower Alley
(leads to school)

YANHE AVENUE

Han River

Yangtze River

REVOLUTION
Is Not a Dinner Party

PART ONE

LITTLE FLOWER

Summer 1972 – Winter 1973

Father's Ponytails

The summer of 1972, before I turned nine, danger began knocking on doors all over China.

My parents worked as doctors in City Hospital Number 4. It was the best hospital in Wuhan, a big city in central China. My father was a surgeon. My mother, a traditional doctor of Chinese medicine, treated patients with herbs and acupuncture needles. When my doll got sick, I treated her with candies.

We lived in a three-story brick building in the hospital compound, near the Yangtze River—the longest river in China. All year round, the river and railroad brought us sweet dates and tea from the East, beautiful silk and candies from the West, tropical fruit from the South, and roasted duck from Beijing, in the North. Father often told me, "Our city is like a human heart—all the body's blood travels through it."

One evening, like many others, the white lace curtains on our open windows danced on the breeze from the courtyard. The sweet smell of roses and the familiar aromas of garlic, ginger, and sesame oil filled our spacious second-floor apartment. We sat around our square table, eating dinner in the living room with its wide picture window that faced the courtyard.

The kitchen and bedrooms were across from the living room. All the rooms on that side had large windows overlooking the rose garden and the walls of the hospital compound.

Mother set a small blue bowl and matching soup-spoon in front of me. "Ling, your hair is as dry as dead grass. Eat your soup." It was filled with tofu, spinach, and seaweed. I didn't want it, but I knew better than to say so. I picked up a bit of tofu, hoping that would be enough. I had already stuffed myself on my favorites: pan-fried dumplings, egg-fried rice, and steamed fish with Mother's tasty black bean sauce. I had even tasted some of the orange sesame chicken, a special treat for Father. Today, though, he

ate only two pieces, leaving most of the chicken in its
serving bowl.

"Hurry, Ling!" Mother said sharply. She was clear-
ing away plates and would want my bowl soon—but
empty. With my eyes, I asked Father if I really had to
eat the awful brown soup.

He smiled the way he always did. Little wrinkles
formed at the corners of his eyes. "It's hot today. You
need the liquid and sodium. At least drink the broth."

Taking a deep breath, I closed my eyes and slurped
down the broth. Blocking the chunks with my teeth,
I made sure none of the slippery seaweed or spinach
got in my mouth.

Mother took the dirty chopsticks and teacups into
the kitchen.

Scooping up the seaweed and spinach in my
spoon, I quickly raised it to Father's mouth. His eyebrows lifted. Then his face relaxed.

"Open please, Daddy!" I whispered.

Father opened up and the yucky greens disappeared. He smacked his lips.

"Love you, Daddy!" I whispered. With two hands, I
carried my bowl to the kitchen.

I was glad Father was home for dinner. When he was around he always saved me from Mother's strange food. On nights when Father performed surgery at the hospital, I had to eat everything Mother thought was good for me: jellyfish would get rid of my freckles; fish tails would help me put on weight; pig's liver would make me smarter; bitter tea would give me smooth skin. All of it tasted horrible. I once told Mother that if we had a dog, even the dog would not eat pig's liver. She rapped my head with her chopsticks and put a second piece in my bowl.

When I returned to the living room, Father still sat at the dinner table, holding a blue porcelain teacup in his hands. The ceiling fan spun slowly above him. His eyes were fixed on the teacup, as if he were studying it.

I didn't like to see him this way. For months Father had been drifting off in thoughts, even in the middle of our English lessons. Wanting to cheer him up, I tiptoed behind him to the bamboo bookshelf that stood next to the wide, brick fireplace. I reached up to the top and took down a yellow magazine with a picture of a human brain on the cover. It had arrived from America last week.

I walked past the fireplace and climbed up onto Father's black chair. It felt wonderful to stretch my sweaty legs across the soft, cool leather.

"Daddy, it's time for ponytails!"

He turned to me and smiled. After setting the teacup beside the matching dishes, he stood and slid his chair under the table, as Mother wanted us to do.

"Read this." I hugged my legs and made room for him.

Father took the magazine and sat beside me. I shifted onto the wide padded armrest and curled up like a little cat. Carefully, I drew together a tuft of his hair, twisted it into a ponytail, and secured it with a red elastic band from my wrist. Father sat still with a grin.

Two years ago, when I turned seven, Mother stopped braiding my hair. She told me I was old enough to do it myself. But I couldn't get it right. My thick, long hair tangled. It was difficult to divide it into three equal parts as my arms grew tired from reaching back. I begged Mother to braid it for me, but she refused, so I wore loose and floppy braids for weeks. Then I came up with the idea of practicing on

Father. His straight hair was much shorter than mine, too short for braids. But I could put ponytails in the front, where it was longest, and practice fastening bands. I worried about hurting him by pulling too hard, but he never complained and always sat still. Though I had mastered ponytails last year, Father still let me practice on him in the evenings when he was home for dinner.

Through the open windows, the warm breeze carried in the voice of a neighbor as she rehearsed a new revolutionary song.

> *Dear Chairman Mao,*
> *Great leader of our country,*
> *The sun in our heart,*
> *You are more dear than our mother and fa-a-a-ther*
> *Fa-a-ther*
> *Fa-a-ther . . .*

She couldn't reach the high note on "father" so she kept trying, "fa-a-ther . . . fa-a-ther," over and over like a broken record.

How could anyone be more dear than my father? Would Chairman Mao let me put ponytails on him? I started to giggle when I pictured ponytails wrapped with red and yellow elastic bands standing on Chairman Mao's square head.

I secured the first band over Father's slippery hair. Would my singing neighbor feel as happy as I was when she could finally reach the high note? I wished she would get there soon—or sing a different song.

Rubbing my nose against the ponytail, I took a deep breath. It smelled of antiseptics, like the hospital. The distinct smell always made him easy to find when we played hide-and-seek.

A sharp crash from our kitchen startled me. The sound of running water continued, but the scraping of a spatula against a wok stopped. My heart sank. Mother had broken another bowl, the second this week. I could picture her breathing deeply and pursing her lips as she held back her anger. Her bad moods always made me nervous. She criticized me more when things went wrong. I was no longer cooled by the chair, and my sleeveless white cotton blouse clung to my sweaty back. Father said that hot weather made everyone short-tempered. But Mother had been like this since last winter.

Father stopped reading. He gently patted my shoulder. As if he knew how I felt, he reached over to the large rectangular radio sitting on the round end table. Instantly, American folk songs filled our apartment. Wiggling to the beat, I felt cheerful again. It must have been six-thirty. That's when Voice of America played a half hour of music between English-language newscasts.

I slipped a pink elastic band off my wrist and wrapped it around Father's second ponytail. He now looked like a clown in the circus.

"Daddy, I'll be nice. I'll only put in two today."

"Don't let me forget about them." Father glanced at his watch. "I have to operate on a patient in two hours, and I don't want to wear ponytails to the hospital again." He burst out laughing. The sound was deep and loud. I joined in his laughter.

"Of course, Daddy." I looked right into his loving eyes. I didn't understand why some children stared at their shoes when talking to their fathers.

Father started my English lessons when I was seven. I hated remembering all the rules of English, such as the s, es, and ies. Yet I had fun pronouncing English words. They sounded like the frogs singing in the field behind the hospital. During my lessons, Father told me stories about America that he had learned from his American teacher. And he taught me English songs and new words and—best of all—I had Father's full attention, with few interruptions from Mother.

We often started our lesson with the picture in the heavy gold frame on the mantel.

We walked to the fireplace. I stood on my tiptoes and reached for the picture. "I'll dust it today, Daddy."

Father took it down and handed it to me.

I slowly ran a blue silk handkerchief over the glass. Inside was a photograph of a long orange bridge with clouds wrapped around it. I dreamed of flying among those clouds.

"Daddy, why are there so many wires on top of the bridge?"

"It helps strengthen the bridge." He took the picture and put it back in the center of the mantel. Picking up the medical journal from the floor under his leather chair, he sat back down.

I climbed in beside him. "It's called—I know, I know—it's called 'sus-pen-sion.'" After carefully saying the difficult English word, I bounced.

"Careful! You'll fall." Father took hold of my arms.

"But you could always stitch me back up, right?" I winked at Father.

Father smiled. "Remember the name of the bridge?"

"Of course! It's called the Golden Gate Bridge in San Francisco, America." I proudly said all this English in a single breath.

"Very good!" Father patted my shoulder.

I had heard the story many times. Dr. Smith gave Father the picture as a farewell present before going back to San Francisco. He had invited Father to go to work in a hospital near the Golden Gate Bridge. But Father decided to stay to help build the new China.

Our entire building used to be Dr. Smith's home. What was now our apartment had been his study and living room. It was here Dr. Smith taught Father and other doctors Western medicine and told them stories about his hometown near the Golden Gate Bridge. Father liked to share those happy times by telling the stories again and again.

"Daddy, I know why you put the picture in a thick golden frame. Because the bridge is heavy!" I burst into laughter.

Father laughed, too.

"Ling," Mother yelled from the kitchen. "How many times do I have to tell you? Don't laugh like that!" Plates clattered in disapproval.

Father covered his mouth with his right hand.

I covered mine quickly, the way Mother had taught me, even though I was no longer laughing. I didn't understand why Father liked my laugh but Mother didn't.

She disapproved of me much of the time. I laughed too loud and forgot to cover my mouth, rudely showing my teeth. I forgot to cross my legs and tuck in my skirt when I sat down. I talked too much. I ate too fast. My feet were too big, and my hair was too dry.

Maybe I could have a good laugh without showing my teeth. But how could I change the size of my feet, which were almost as big as hers? And what could I do about my dry, tangled hair? I ate fast because I loved to eat. If I took small bites like Mother, it would take all night for me to finish dinner. Or I would be hungry all the time. I wished she loved me the way I was, like Father did.

I believed Mother was unhappy with me because she had never wanted to have a daughter. She told our neighbor Mrs. Wong if she were younger she would try to have a son.

But Father loved me. I was his special girl.

Mother walked into the living room with a bamboo tray. I glanced at her as she moved closer to the dinner table. Her white lace apron covered her slender waist and part of her black silk dress. As always, her silky black hair was neatly pinned back, with every hair in place. Her pearl necklace shone in the last bit of summer sunlight coming through the windows. I could smell her jasmine perfume from across the room. She was more beautiful than the lady on the jars of powdered milk sent to us by Father's friends in America. How could I ever be as beautiful and perfect as she was?

Mother narrowed her eyes as she looked at me. "Ling, you are too old to play with your father's hair. Take the ponytails out right after your lesson."

My stomach tightened. It was Father's hair, and he hadn't told me I was too old.

Mother set the blue rice bowls covered with small lotus flowers on the tray, one at a time. I still remembered how hard she scolded me when I stacked the bowls together.

How could I learn every one of Mother's rules so I wouldn't upset her?

As soon as Mother left the room, Father patted my back. He whispered, "Your mother has a lot on her mind these days. Be patient with her. Let's start our new words for today."

I wanted to ask Father what was on Mother's mind. Was it because she wanted a boy? But I was afraid she would hear my questions from the kitchen.

I worked hard to pronounce new English words after Father. "Pick, pike, big, beg, dig." I imagined father and daughter frogs singing in a pond.

"Fountain, mountain . . ."

Looking up at him, I burst out laughing again. I had forgotten about his ponytails.

Waste Is a Great Crime

Summer ended with three weeks of nonstop rain. Everything smelled of mold. When I walked through the muddy streets, I tried not to step on the political posters the rain had washed off the walls. I hated getting my hands dirty peeling the grimy paper off my shoes.

Mother replaced the bamboo mat on my bed with cotton bedding.

On a gray fall afternoon, a strange man and woman came to our apartment while Father was at work. Mother introduced the woman as the Communist Party secretary for the city and the man as Comrade Li.

The woman had short legs and long arms. Her baggy blue pants were rolled up above her brown rubber boots. She and Comrade Li did not take off their shoes and walked around our apartment leaving mud stains all over the floor.

When they crossed the living room to the fire-place, the Secretary Lady tapped her broken finger-nail against our blue flower vase on the mantel. "Did this come from overseas?" she asked in a nasal voice.

Without waiting for Mother's answer, she turned and went into my parents' bedroom. Comrade Li followed. His blue army pants hung on him like flat balloons. There she opened the wardrobe and rubbed the fabric of Mother's dresses between her thick fingers.

Leaving the wardrobe open, they walked into my room. She brushed her hand over the yellow silk comforter on my bed. Her calluses caught at the pink embroidered peonies.

I stayed close to Mother as she followed behind them. She wore the smile she gave only to visitors, but she kept rubbing the third button on her white shirt, something she did when she was nervous.

As the Secretary Lady walked toward the kitchen, she waved at Comrade Li. "Come here. Don't let me do all the work."

Once in the kitchen, Comrade Li used a chopstick

to poke and stir inside our rice jar. In Father's study, he picked up Father's ivory cigarette holder from the bookcase and squeezed it as if he expected a cigarette to pop out. Maybe he had never seen one before. It was a special gift to Father from Dr. Smith in America.

The Secretary Lady turned several of Father's books upside down and shook them. Notes and bookmarks fell to the floor like dead leaves. She pointed at them. "Take those with us," she ordered.

Comrade Li bent down and scooped up the little pieces of paper, stuffing them into the big pockets of his army jacket.

The notes were written in English. I wasn't sure why she wanted them. Father had spent many hours reading those books and taking notes. I bet he wouldn't be happy if he saw Comrade Li crumpling them up like that.

"Check all the shoes," said the Secretary Lady.

At the entryway, Comrade Li picked up Father's brown leather shoes from the rack. He tapped the heels with his knuckles and peeked inside before putting them back. What could he be looking for?

As soon as they left, Mother locked the door and threw all the clothes they had touched in a washbasin, even her silk robe. I asked if it was because they had dirty hands. She hissed and said, "No questions now!"

If Mother didn't want them to touch our things, why didn't she stop them?

That weekend Father moved the furniture and books out of the study. He jammed the books into the bookcases around the fireplace. Mother told me Comrade Li was going to live in Father's study.

As Father nailed shut the door between his study and our living room, I asked, "Who is Comrade Li? Why are you letting him move in?"

With a serious look on his face, Father continued pounding at a long nail. "He is the new political officer for the hospital, and he needs a place to stay."

"What does a political officer do?" I asked.

"He teaches Chairman Mao's ideas. Now let me finish what I'm doing." Looking stern, he screwed a brass latch onto the upper half of the study door. I knew better than to ask more questions.

So Comrade Li was a teacher? Would Father have to take lessons from him? But how could anyone be smarter than Father?

The following week, Father's study became Comrade Li's home. To get into his new apartment, Comrade Li knocked out part of the wall facing the stairway landing and installed a new door. He pasted Chairman Mao's teachings all over the door. It looked like one of the political study boards that were hanging throughout the city.

I worried Comrade Li would often pick through our things, but he didn't come to our home again that fall. He greeted me nicely when I passed him in the hallway. One good thing was that Mother stopped scolding me loudly. Soon I got used to him living next to us.

When the first snow covered the ground, Comrade Li wrote one of Chairman Mao's teachings on a big poster and pasted it to the side of our building.

WASTE IS A GREAT CRIME.
SAVE RESOURCES TO BUILD A NEW CHINA.

The next day, someone shut down the boiler in the basement and we no longer had heat or hot water in our building. Our apartment was so cold we had to wear layers of heavy cotton jackets throughout the day.

The worst part was bathing. Once a week, Mother boiled hot water on the stove and mixed it with cold water in a big wooden tub for my bath. As soon as I took off my winter clothes, I was covered with goose bumps. If the water was too hot, I had to wait to get in. If the water was cool enough to get in, it turned cold before Mother finished soaping me up.

I fought taking baths until one day Mrs. Wong, our upstairs neighbor, heard our argument. She invited me to bathe in her bathroom, where they had a real tub and an airplane-shaped electric heater to keep the room warm. After that, every Saturday I was a happy little dumpling, floating in warm soup.

The Wongs were the only family in the compound who had an electric heater. Mrs. Wong had bought it after Comrade Li cut off the heat. Many neighbors from around the courtyard went to see it. No one had ever seen one before. Comrade Li was not happy about it. He never went to see the heater, and I heard him tell neighbors that someday he would take their heater. I thought that sounded silly. The Wongs wouldn't let him take their heater. Whenever they passed each other, Dr. Wong looked past Comrade Li, and Mrs. Wong turned her head away.

When I asked Mother why the Wongs didn't like Comrade Li, she said sternly, "Who told you that? Don't ever talk like that again."

"Can we buy a heater?" I asked.

Mother pointed a finger upward toward the Wongs' apartment. "Only a family that has relatives overseas can afford expensive things like that." Dr. Wong's brother sent them money and packages from Hong Kong every week. We used to receive letters from overseas, too, but at the beginning of winter, after receiving a letter that had been opened, Mother became nervous and told Father to stop writing to his friends.

Why would anyone want to open our letters? Did they hope to find money? If they knew that Father's friends never sent us money, would they stop?

One time when I walked by Comrade Li's apartment, his door was open. I peeked in and saw a stack of letters on his chair. The one on top was addressed to the dentist who had fixed my cavity, and had recently been declared as a people's enemy.

Comrade Li couldn't be the one opening our letters, could he?

Bartering with Comrade Li

As the weather grew warmer in the spring of 1973, the power in our building kept going out. The second time this happened on a hot afternoon, I left our apartment to see if I could find someplace cooler. As I walked down the stairs, Comrade Li greeted me from the landing.

"How are you today, Ling?" he said with his monkey grin.

"Hello, Comrade Li." Since Mother was not with me, I decided it would be all right to talk to him. "I'm so hot! The electricity is out again. Without the fan, my heat rash itches me to death."

"You need to grow outside your greenhouse, little flower!" He scratched his neck. "We must endure small pains and hardships to build a new China."

I wanted to tell him that my heat rash was not a small pain, but Mother had taught me that it was not polite to talk back to adults.

"The electricity saved is used to make more iron and steel for the Revolution." He waved his hand like a magician. "Soon we will be the next superpower!"

"What's a superpower?" I asked.

He laughed loudly. "A mighty nation that has everything we need, especially electricity!"

"Really?" I asked.

I was about to ask how soon we could be a super-power, when he said, "We can't have our little flower drooping, can we? I will see what we can do to speed up our Revolution."

I gave him my nice smile and thanked him. I couldn't wait to have electricity again in our apartment.

By now, my English had improved and I knew how to write and say many short sentences. I had been cut-ting out pictures of animals, people, houses, food, and flowers from Father's old magazines. I pasted them onto paper to make little books.

One night as Father listened to Voice of America, I read my little book *A Story About a Happy Girl*.

A girl lives near the Golden Gate Bridge.
She wears a pretty red dress.
She has curly brown hair.
She has big eyes.
She likes to eat ice cream.
She plays with her dog on the green lawn.

KNOCK! KNOCK-KNOCK-KNOCK.

It was the secret code I shared with Comrade Li.

As I ran to the door that separated our living room from his home, Father snapped off the radio.

The upper part of the brown wood door had a smaller door cut into it. We could unlock it using a latch on our side. While I opened the little door, Father slid his medical journal under his chair and picked up a newspaper.

A few months ago Comrade Li had lightly rapped on the door and gave me a folded paper swan. He asked for an apple in return. And that was how we started our "buying and selling" game.

Now whenever he needed a few eggs, green onions,

cooking oil, or a needle and thread, he knocked on the little door. I gave him what he asked for, and he paid me with origami.

"Hello." I stood on my toes. "What would you like to buy today?"

"Some eggs and a few green onions. How much do I owe you?" He spoke in Mandarin, blurred with a northern countryside accent. Comrade Li had magic hands. He could fold paper into anything—flowers, boats, birds, and even a bucket with two handles. He also knew magic tricks, like how to make a ten-fen coin disappear or turn into one fen.

"One bird, please!" I showed him my index finger. Sometimes I wished he would pay me with something besides origami. I already had a basketful. But I did not dare tell him that. Mother would be upset with me.

"Right away!" He blinked his tiny, black sesame seed eyes.

Standing on tiptoe, I peeked through the open door as Comrade Li went to the round table in the middle of his room. The table and its straight-backed chair were always covered with piles of posters, letters, rolls of paper, dozens of brushes, and bottles of red and black ink. He picked up a piece of white paper and came back.

"Keep your eyes open, so you can see the bird grow." His laugh sounded like a happy goose.

Comrade Li creased the paper to make a triangle and then brought up one corner to make the bird's neck. Flip! Flip! Flip! And all at once, he was holding a lively bird.

"Hold it tight so it won't fly away!" He handed it to me. It had a long beak and big wings.

"I will be right back." Holding the bird with both hands, I skipped to my room next to the kitchen and set it in the basket.

As I dashed around the corner to the kitchen, I almost bumped into Mother. She was carrying a crystal plate piled with mango slices. I started to reach for a slice of sweet-smelling mango when Mother said in her low, firm voice, "Don't run like that. Be a lady."

I pulled my hand back, hoping Comrade Li hadn't heard Mother scolding me. How could anyone like me if they heard my mother scold me all the time?

Mother set the tray on the dinner table and followed me to the kitchen. I was surprised to see her yellow rubber gloves floating in the soapy water in the sink. She must have taken them off in a hurry. She would have yelled at me if I'd left them there.

"I'll get the eggs." Mother bent over and snatched two eggs with one hand from a half-full bamboo basket. Small beads of sweat on her forehead shone in the kitchen lights.

I grabbed a few green onions from a vegetable basket on the counter. With my other hand, I reached down and picked up another egg. Last time, when I sold Comrade Li two eggs, he said he needed one more to make a meal.

Mother reached over to support the egg I was holding.

I wriggled out of her reach. I didn't want Comrade Li to think I wasn't even old enough to carry one small egg!

Mother gave me the squinty eye. I pretended not to see it.

When Mother and I came out of the kitchen, Comrade Li had stretched his head through the little door into our living room, like a turtle coming out of its shell. Father didn't seem to notice Comrade Li. He tapped the fingers of his left hand gently on the arm of his chair, keeping his newspaper folded in half and close to his face.

When he saw Mother and me, Comrade Li drew his head back into his apartment.

Standing on tiptoe, I passed the egg through the door and peered again into his apartment. It smelled of garlic and ink. A bed stood against the white wall across the room. The wall above was covered with photos. On one end of his bed sat a green blanket, folded neatly into a square like a giant green mung bean cookie. His blue cap sat on top. Comrade Li had told me that in the army everyone could make his bed in less than three minutes.

Being in the army must have given him lots of friends. The wooden door between our homes couldn't block out the loud conversations he had with his many visitors. He told them about his life in the army and the important people who stood beside him in his photos. He bragged the most about a large picture hanging in the center, a place of honor.

He had once proudly pointed it out to me and Mother. "This is Comrade Jiang Qing, the wife of our great leader, Chairman Mao."

In the picture, Comrade Li and five other men stood around a small woman. They were all dressed in Mao-style blue army uniforms and wore caps with short visors. The woman had her hair cut above her ears. Even from my side of the door, I saw her fierce eyes behind the glasses. They made me think about a hungry ghost in one of my books.

Now Mother passed Comrade Li the other eggs and the green onions. "You haven't had dinner yet?" Her voice had the same tone she used when scolding me, but she wore her smile for visitors.

"Not yet, Dr. Xiong." Everyone used Mother's maiden name. I guess it would be too confusing to have two Dr. Changs in one family. "We had to get ready to arrest an undercover enemy." He cocked his head like a proud rooster.

"What's an undercover enemy?" I asked.

Mother pinched me on the back of the arm. Ow! Comrade Li glanced at Father, then leaned forward. His tiny eyes glared into mine. "Someone who seems to be nice but works to destroy our government," he whispered.

Why would anyone want to destroy our government? I wished to ask what he would do after he arrested the enemy, but I didn't want to risk getting another pinch.

"Do you need anything else?" asked Mother, the smile on her face disappearing.

Comrade Li stretched his head out again. Mother pulled me to the side. He glanced around, then fixed his eyes on our dinner table.

"Some young revolutionaries are coming here tonight. They would enjoy the mangoes." He pointed his chin toward the table and smiled, showing off his tobacco-stained buckteeth.

Without a word, Mother went to the table and carried the plate over.

I was too shocked to cry out. I loved mangoes! They were so expensive, and it had been a long time since we'd had them. If only Mother had hidden the mangoes, the way she hid the chocolate and coffee from him.

Comrade Li took the plate from Mother and carried it to the table in the middle of his room. As he walked back to the little door, he pressed his hand to his scalp, flattening a few greasy hairs that stood up on his monkey head. "Oh, come closer, Ling. There's something in your ear." He reached his arm out.

I stepped forward and held my breath as his greasy sleeve passed by my cheek. He plucked something from behind my ear.

"This is for you!"

He held a small red paper bag. My mouth fell open. This was the first time he had given me anything other than origami.

Inside was a portrait of Chairman Mao on a palm-sized metal button. Chairman Mao wore the same blue army jacket as Comrade Li. I had never seen a button like this one.

"Thank you! Thank you!" I jumped up and down. It almost made up for losing dessert.

Mother gave me a stern look.

All summer the children in the courtyard were showing off their button collections. I couldn't wait to trade this one for the ceramic button of Chairman Mao holding an umbrella. Maybe from now on, Comrade Li would always pay me with Mao's buttons instead of origami.

"It's a new release. The whole hospital got only

ten. Put it on your shirt." Comrade Li stuck out his chest. He had the same button pinned on the right side of his shirt.

"Ling will put it on after her shower. Good-bye." Mother took the button away from me. With one hand behind my neck, she firmly moved me away from him. I worried that Comrade Li could hear the upset in her voice. Mother closed the door and hooked the latch. She turned toward Father and wrinkled her face as if she had just eaten a moldy peanut.

Father quickly crossed the room. "You did fine." He patted her shoulder. "Hopefully the mangoes will keep him busy for the night." Father wrapped his arms around her.

I thought my parents did not like Comrade Li because he bought things from us. I was wrong.

Homemade Ice Cream
and German Chocolate

We didn't have a real shower in our apartment. Mother attached a hose to the faucet in the kitchen. She tied the other end to a water pipe that ran up to the ceiling. It hung over a drain in the corner of our concrete floor. This became our shower.

Each day of summer, I looked forward to getting in the cold shower after dinner. I stayed in as long as I could.

"Hurry up, Ling. I have the ointment ready for you." Mother opened the kitchen door a crack.

"I'm drying off." I quickly turned off the water and wrapped myself in a big towel decorated with a red rose print.

Mother came in. With a cotton ball, she swabbed a white, cooling mint ointment all over my neck, arms, and legs. It felt like she had blown magic cold air onto my heat rash. The itching stopped for a minute. I wished my skin could feel this way the rest of the day. In the mirror hanging next to the kitchen window, I saw an oval-faced porcelain doll with patches. I stretched wide my double-lidded eyes and wobbled my head. If we could just run our fan more often. What was taking the Revolution so long?

As I dressed, I heard Father greeting someone. "Come in! Come in, please!"

A soft voice asked, "Where is my sweet girl?" It was Mrs. Wong! I quickly buttoned my cotton blouse and ran out of the kitchen. Dr. Wong, Mrs. Wong, and their son, Niu, were here. The Wongs had just returned from shopping. A big yellow straw bag sat by our front door.

"Here I am!" I stretched out my arms and wrapped them around Mrs. Wong's waist. When she bent down to kiss my cheek, her long, wavy hair tickled my nose and smelled of jasmine tea. I once overheard her tell Mother she used pearl powder to wash her face and tea to rinse her hair. She had to be the most beautiful lady in the world. Today she wore a red silk top with ruffles all down the front and a big full skirt with red and green flowers.

Behind her stood Dr. Wong and Niu. Dr. Wong wore a light yellow shirt, white shorts, and a pair of white leather shoes. He was not as tall as Father, but had the same wide shoulders and dark skin. He looked like a tennis player from Father's English magazines.

"Is this a good time to visit?" With one finger, Dr. Wong pushed up his gold-framed glasses. He glanced at Comrade Li's apartment.

Father shrugged. "Let me show you this article." He led Dr. Wong to our dinner table.

Niu's short-sleeved white shirt was tucked into his long blue trousers. He walked over to Father's book-case and pulled out a music book. Mrs. Wong complained to Mother that Niu refused to wear shorts, no matter how hot it was. I guessed that was because he didn't want his skinny chopstick legs to show.

"Let me take a good look at you, my little doll." Mrs. Wong bent down on one knee. She pulled back my collar to examine my neck.

"My poor thing! You shouldn't wear a blouse with a collar anymore, it makes your rash worse." Her big brown eyes widened. "Come upstairs. We'll pick out a fabric and I'll sew you a new blouse."

I felt as if she had just handed me a bag of ginger candy. I looked at Mother for approval. The smile faded from her face.

I hoped she'd let me go.

Mrs. Wong had told Mother many times that she dreamed of having a daughter like me. Sometimes I wondered if Mother would be as nice if she stayed home like Mrs. Wong did. Yet Mother often told Father she couldn't imagine wasting her years of schooling to be just a housewife.

"Thank you, Mrs. Wong," said Mother. "On such a hot day, we don't want to trouble you."

"No trouble! Why don't you all come up and have ice cream? I made some yesterday after the electricity came back on." She picked up the big shopping bag. Niu snapped shut Father's music book, *Romantic Songs from Russia*, and slipped it back onto the shelf. He could sing half the songs in that book.

My eyes begged Mother.

"All right, Ling. You can go for a while. I'm afraid I have to stay here and write up reports for new patients." Mother straightened my collar. The rash around my neck itched and burned again. "You behave!"

Whenever Mother and Mrs. Wong were together they reminded me of flowers in our courtyard garden. Mother was like a proud white rose, which stood alone. I was afraid to touch her because of her thorns. Mrs. Wong was fragrant and warm like a red peony, which always welcomed visitors. I wanted to be close to her.

I glanced at Father, hoping he would go. He loved ice cream almost as much as I did. Father looked up. "No, thank you. I have to go to the hospital soon."

Dr. Wong didn't even look up from the magazine. "You know I don't care for sweets," he said as he continued reading. "And I have to go to the hospital, too."

I was afraid of Dr. Wong. His eyes never smiled from behind his gold-framed glasses. Unlike Father, he made no jokes. His smell reminded me of small plum flowers with pink petals, the only flower that blossomed in our courtyard on cold snowy days. Behind their backs, I had heard the nurses call Father and Dr. Wong "the two handsome surgeons, Dr. Warm and Dr. Cold." Though they were very different,

Father and Dr. Wong were good friends. Both of them had been Dr. Smith's favorite students. They would chat in English over tea for hours. Patients came from all over the country seeking their help. One from northern China had traveled two days to see them.

"Well, let's go have ice cream, then. Who is coming?" Mrs. Wong looked at me and smiled.

My eyes followed Niu as he edged toward the door. I moved in front of him and yelled, "You can only beat me in your dreams!" I jabbed him with an elbow as we crowded through the doorway.

"Ling!" Mother's scolding chased me up the stairs, along with Niu. "Be a lady!"

"Niu, you're losing again!" Mrs. Wong's tinkling laugh echoed along the staircase.

Barely beating Niu, I slapped the gold lion knocker on the heavy red door. "Touched base!" Turning back, I smiled proudly at him.

Niu's pale face had turned red. His glasses had slipped down on his nose. "Oh, I let you win. You know I am a nice brother." He pushed back his glasses.

Niu was four years older than I was. I barely reached his shoulder. All the kids living around the courtyard knew I had a "big brother," even though he didn't live with us. Whenever I played with him in the courtyard, I felt safe and protected. Father always said when I was born he was happy to have a daughter, because he already had a son—Niu.

I thought Niu was the luckiest boy in China. Along with having a real bathtub, a heater, and a refrigerator, his family was the only one I knew who owned a sewing machine.

"Niu, get the bowls ready. I'll get the ice cream out in a minute." Mrs. Wong set the shopping bag on the redwood table in the middle of their living room. "Come here, Ling. Let me show you some fabric." She led me to the sandalwood dresser beside the bathroom. It was decorated with carvings of a phoenix. The top shelf held layers of blankets. The middle shelf was full of colorful sweaters. She kept all her sewing fabric on the bottom shelf.

"Which would you like for your new blouse?" She dabbed her forehead with the tip of her white handkerchief.

I stood there staring at the stack of beautiful fabric, not sure what to do. Should I be polite and say, "*No,*

thank you. It's too much trouble," like Mother often did?
But I really wanted to have a new blouse.

"Don't be shy." Mrs. Wong took out a stack of fabric and held it in front of me. "Take your pick."

I pointed to a thin cotton fabric with the same pattern as her bathroom curtains—little girls in red sun hats sitting on a beach. Behind them were palm trees and sailboats floating on water. Above them were the moon and stars. The pattern reminded me of pictures from Father's hometown on Hainan Island, far away in southern China.

Whenever I saw the curtains, I daydreamed about going to a beach in southern China and picking up seashells with Father.

"All right, my dear. We have enough material to make you a blouse." She handed me the fabric and put the rest inside the chest.

I followed Mrs. Wong into the kitchen to her foot-pedal sewing machine. The beautiful black-and-silver machine had been an anniversary present from Dr. Wong. Mrs. Wong was almost as proud of her new machine as she was of her heater. It stood in the corner of the kitchen, where she could look out on the Han River beyond our courtyard. The kitchen's tall French doors led to a patio.

The Wongs' apartment was much bigger than ours. For one thing, the corner of their apartment wasn't someone else's home. For another, their bathroom was in their apartment, instead of down the hall, like ours.

"Can we have ice cream now?" Niu asked. He pulled out the chair next to him for me, drumming his long fingers on the table.

I was glad he asked first. I couldn't wait to have the cold ice cream melting in my mouth.

Sitting next to Niu at the small kitchen table, I could smell the fragrant detergent from his clothes. I studied his face. He had Dr. Wong's single-lidded eyes and Mrs. Wong's full lips. Unlike other boys in the courtyard, he always dressed nice and clean.

"Be patient," said Mrs. Wong. She walked to the refrigerator by the French doors, twisting up her hair into a bun. I stared at her porcelain neck and wondered why she never got heat rash.

An evening breeze drifted in from the Han River. It had been a rainy spring, so the river now filled its banks with dark green water. A few blocks down, it joined the wide, light brown Yangtze. The setting sun turned the smooth river into a golden blanket. On the left stood the Han Bridge. Lines of cars and bicycles moved slowly along it. On the right, a row of short buildings crowded together. The three buildings in our courtyard were the tallest in the neighborhood.

Mrs. Wong told me that our building was the oldest in the courtyard. The other two buildings were built after the Communist revolution, with small apartments.

From our apartment, the milk trees blocked the view. Niu and I gave that name to the trees around our building because if we picked one of the leaves, white liquid flowed from the stem. I licked it once, and the milk tasted bitter.

Mrs. Wong brought us two glass bowls on matching saucers. In each bowl sat three scoops of red bean ice cream. Square chocolates rested on the sides of each saucer.

I took a small bite of the ice cream. Wishing to keep the sweet taste in my mouth as long as I could, I waited until it melted before swallowing it.

Niu picked up the chocolate and looked at the foreign letters on the plastic candy wrapper.

"Is this English?" I asked.

"No, this is obviously German." He slid his wrapper over to me. "They make good chocolate."

"Oh, all chocolate tastes good to me."

I took the wrapper and smoothed it out. I didn't like it when Niu talked to me as if I was a little kid, but I put up with it because he always gave me his wrappers.

The kids at school prized these colorful plastic wrappers. They were hard to come by, since most candy was wrapped in paper. We used them as bookmarks or placed white paper over them to trace the drawings. After collecting a few, I could trade them for things like postcard portraits of Chairman Mao. I could then trade the postcards for homemade hairpins or even small handkerchiefs with stitched-on flowers.

A small barge blew its horn, sounding like a mooing cow. I pointed at the river.

"Where are the boats headed? Are they going to San Francisco?"

Niu rolled his eyes in exasperation. "Those are riverboats. They would never make it across the great Pacific."

I hummed. I bet Niu learned to talk like that from Dr. Wong.

Niu stared at the river and took another bite of ice cream. "You need to do better with your geography. Remind me to show you my maps."

"Ling is not quite ten yet. She will learn," interrupted Mrs. Wong.

Niu frowned at his mother and continued, "I need to show her how far away San Francisco is. She is very confused." He shook his head. "It's a lot of work to be her brother."

I wanted to tell him I didn't like maps. I could never find the place I was looking for. But I held back. Out the window, Gardener Zong's bald head bobbed up and down. He was planting more flowers along the walkway to our building. He always kept the garden tidy.

Mrs. Wong pulled a chair up behind me and combed my hair. She was gentle. It didn't hurt the way it often did with Mother.

"Let's put your beautiful hair up so you will feel cooler."

I nodded and my heart grew. Mother never told me my hair was beautiful. Niu only stared. Did he think I had beautiful hair? Did he think I was beautiful?

Mrs. Wong made two tight braids and pinned them around my head, just like the French girl from a painting in her living room.

After ice cream, Niu and I took turns playing his silver harmonica. He could play many songs, even the new revolutionary ones. I couldn't even play scales. I lost interest.

"What do you want to be when you grow up?" I wiped off the harmonica with the corner of my blouse before handing it to him.

"A surgeon," Niu answered without hesitation. "What about you?"

For a moment I couldn't remember my latest plan. I had wanted to be a juice bar saleslady. Then I could sell red bean juice bars to my parents so they wouldn't have to wait in line. I had also wanted to be a clerk in a fabric store. I'd save all the pretty fabric for Mrs. Wong. And I had wanted to be a ticket lady at a movie theater, so I could let Niu in, even when he had no ticket. But the plan that stayed with me longest was to become a teacher. I'd send home all the kids in my class who had dirty faces and runny noses.

"I want to be a teacher," I said. But I didn't tell him why.

"Not a bad choice for a girl, I guess," said Niu. Mrs. Wong gave me an approving smile.

I wiggled happily in my chair and grinned at Niu. He flipped through the music book for another song to play. He was serious like Dr. Wong. Why couldn't he be more cheerful like Mrs. Wong?

Mrs. Wong spread the fabric out on the table and drew yellow lines on it with a piece of chalk. She had designed and sewn Mother's red wedding dress. Mother looked like a fairy in its high collar, flowing sleeves, and long skirt. Whenever I looked at the wedding picture hanging in my parents' bedroom, I dreamed that one day I would wear the same dress and marry a surgeon as handsome as Father.

I watched Niu thoughtfully. His glasses looked funny. I doubted he would ever let me put ponytails in his hair. I decided I had to find someone else to marry.

Suddenly, I heard shouts and car doors slamming. Niu ran to the patio. Mrs. Wong and I followed.

"What's happening?" asked Niu.

A green jeep stopped in front of the apartment building across the courtyard. Comrade Li and three teenage boys ran inside. We heard doors banging, dishes breaking, and someone screaming.

"Something bad is happening! Let's get inside," urged Mrs. Wong. Niu and I didn't move, so she stood behind, wrapping her arms around us.

A few moments later, Comrade Li and the boys pushed someone out of the building.

"They're arresting an undercover enemy," I said. My heart pounded.

"What undercover enemy? Who is it?" Niu asked.

I scrunched part of my white skirt into my fist. We couldn't see the enemy's face. A white pillowcase with the red words NUMBER 4 HOSPITAL covered it. It must have been a lady. One of her purple slippers was left outside the building. Her head jerked from side to side as Comrade Li and the boys shoved her into the jeep.

Sweat rolled down my back. Before this, I had seen people being arrested only in revolutionary movies.

Were they going to torture her, like the evil people did to communist revolutionary heroes? Would she be as brave as the heroes were in the movies and not tell her secrets?

I heard loud tapping on the Wongs' fireplace pipe. Running over, I called down, "Yes, Mother." Our fireplace shared the same pipe as the Wongs'. Since we had no telephone, when the two families needed to talk we tapped on the pipe.

"Come home now!" Mother's order echoed up.

Mrs. Wong and Niu walked me to the door. She kissed me on my cheeks and whispered in my ear as always, "I wish you were my daughter." My heart burst with the same wish.

As I waved good-bye to them, I saw tears in her eyes.

"Bloodsucking Landlord!"

My heat rash was no longer red and itchy as the milk tree leaves began to turn shades of yellow and orange. Since I had the highest test scores at the end of third grade, Teacher Hui, who taught Chinese literature, had recommended to the school board that I skip fourth grade. I looked forward to starting fifth grade. Even though I would be the youngest in the class, I was sure I'd still be the first one to raise a hand to answer her questions.

Teacher Hui was slender and shorter than Mother and Mrs. Wong. She had a perm in her shoulder-length hair. She could wear a blue scarf many different ways. She often read my writing to the class as she slowly walked between the rows of desks. Once in a while, her beautiful double-lidded eyes would smile at me. I liked the way she bent her fingers and pushed her curly hair behind her ears.

On the first day of the new school year, singing birds outside my window woke me early. I slipped into an outfit with the big red and white flowers that matched the one my doll Bao-bao wore. This was one of three matching outfits Mrs. Wong had made for us. Bao-bao was my only doll. Dr. Smith sent her to me one Christmas. Her big eyes closed when I laid her down for a nap. When I patted her tummy, she made happy, gurgling sounds.

I gave Bao-bao a good-bye kiss and slipped my purple schoolbag strap over my shoulder. Following Mother out the door, I ran my fingers over the big yellow butterfly on the front of my bag.

Unlike other mornings, I didn't hear Comrade Li singing. He loved to sing Jiang Qing's revolutionary operas. We always knew when he was in the bathroom. He sang from when he went in until he flushed the toilet. Father joked that his singing sounded like a strangled ghost. I hated to hear Comrade Li start, because it meant I had to rush to get ready for school.

Mother and I passed by Comrade Li's door. It was open wide, but he wasn't inside. In the middle of the courtyard, he led a group of neighbors in a Zhong, a loyalty dancing class to show their love for Chairman Mao. In front of them hung a giant portrait of Mao in a big wooden frame, neon lights stretched outward from him, as though he were a burning sun.

Comrade Li sang through a loudspeaker while the group chitchatted.

> Great teacher, great leader,
> You are the sun in all our hearts,
> Dear Chairman Mao.
> Long live Chairman Mao.
> Long live, long live, long live, long live Chairman Mao!

Neighbors waved their hands above their heads and kicked their feet from side to side. Old ladies in the back gossiped as they danced. Old men puffed on hand-rolled cigarettes, and little boys waved canes and sticks like swords.

I wondered if the family of the undercover enemy was among them. It had been weeks since the arrest, but no one ever talked about it. When I questioned

my parents, Mother gave me her disapproving look.
Father said, "It is grown-up business."

Comrade Li's voice broke on the high notes.
Young nurses giggled. He continued:

> Long live Chairman Mao!
> Long live, long live Chairman Mao!

One young doctor sent his slipper flying right
past me. Red-faced, he ran over to get it back. I
wished I could stay to join the class. Then I could
show off my ballet turns. But I didn't want to be late
for school.

When we walked by the milk trees lining the courtyard, I plucked a leaf and licked the sap. Mother
glared at me, but I was too happy to care. The milk
even tasted a bit sweet today. I was going to be in a
class with older kids. None of them would have runny
noses.

Mother said I was old enough to go to school by
myself. She and I had made a few practice walks. The
compound gate opened onto busy Victory Road.
Across that road was the hospital. Between home and
school, only Victory Road was wide enough for cars.

The rest of my way was through a short, narrow alley. Mother stopped at the left turn to Flower Alley.

"Come home as soon as morning classes are over," she said. "And don't talk to strangers."

Nodding cheerfully, I skipped down the alley. In my mind, I practiced introducing myself to my new classmates. "Hello, I'm Ling. I'm glad to meet you. What's your name?" Or, "Hello, what's your name? Mine is Ling."

I felt grown up now that I could walk to school by myself. During outings with Father to the park or the pastry shop, he had told me about the history of the city. Before Chairman Mao's Communists took over, many foreigners lived here. They built the wide-paved streets lined with schools, churches, modern hospitals, tall office buildings, and fancy apartment buildings with kitchens and bathrooms. It was as if someone had picked up buildings from Western countries and scattered them all around the city. To celebrate the victory of the Communist Revolution, many of the streets had been renamed, such as Big Liberation Road, Victory Road, Workers and Parents Road, and Red Five Stars Road.

Along these streets, walls were covered with huge murals. Chairman Mao's portraits, red flags, and posters of his teachings were in every corner of the city.

All the Westerners were gone now. When I thought about San Francisco, I wondered what kind of murals they had of their leader. Did he also wear a funny hat like Chairman Mao?

As I walked around the city with my parents, one moment we'd be among large Western-style buildings, and the next in one of many narrow stone-paved alleys. These older alleys were lined with single-story houses with low roofs. In warm weather, their doors were open. Families crowded inside. They had no bathrooms. When I used our large, clean bathroom, I often felt sorry for those people who had to walk blocks to use dirty public bathrooms like the one at the end of Flower Alley.

I went in once and found there were no toilets, only holes in the ground. One girl squatted over a hole, reading a picture book, as if the smell didn't bother her at all. The stink forced me to run right out.

Pinching my nose with my flowered handkerchief until I was well past the public bathroom, I turned right at the end of the alley. There stood the school's iron gates, painted bright blue. In front of the open gates, noisy boys and girls crowded around an old lady with white hair and a wrinkled face. A rope that looped behind her neck held up a small wooden tray in front of her. She was selling five-spiced water-melon seeds, rice candy, and two-inch-long purple sugar canes. Mother would never allow me to buy anything from street vendors. She said the treats were covered with germs.

Squeezing through the crowd, I ran inside the school courtyard. Three boys from my old third-grade class were dribbling white liquid from tea-kettles onto the ground, drawing lines for a basketball game. They stopped when they saw me. I smiled at them. They grinned and looked away.

A big cloth picture of Chairman Mao with a group of Young Pioneers hung from the three-story building. In it, the Young Pioneers huddled around Chairman Mao as he extended his arms over them. I thought of baby ducklings and an old duck. I looked forward to joining the Young Pioneers and wearing a red scarf around my neck, just like the older kids in the courtyard. I had used Father's red silk tie to practice making the knot.

I found my name on the list beside the second classroom on the first floor. Someone tapped my shoulder. It was Hong, my friend from third grade. Her smile dimpled her round cheeks.

"So are you really skipping a grade?" she asked.

I nodded.

"I'll miss you," she said.

"We can still play together." I patted her arm. "I have to go now."

I couldn't wait to meet my new classmates. Taking a deep breath, I walked in. Rows of wooden desks and long benches filled the room. A group of boys and girls stood near the door beside the blackboard. Although I was skipping only one grade, the fifth-graders were much taller and bigger than I was. Half were dressed in Mao's army uniforms and wore red scarves. I forgot the greetings I had practiced.

A girl with dark skin standing in the center of the crowd called out, "Look, look, here comes the blood-sucking landlord!" The crowd turned toward me and laughed loudly. I froze. The girl's short hair barely showed under her blue cap. Her blue shirt and pants had different-colored patches at the elbows and knees. She wore an old pair of army shoes with her big toes sticking out. She looked like a peasant.

"I bet she can crow like a rooster," said a rabbit-faced fat boy. The brass buttons on his new Mao's uniform shone in the sunlight. My face burned. Another wave of laughter filled the room.

They were comparing me to the landlord in the movie *Midnight Rooster*. I had seen it last summer when it was playing in all the theaters. In the movie, the cruel landlord always wore an outfit with large flowers. She and her husband ordered the workers to get up when the rooster crowed. At midnight, she crowed like a rooster, tricking the peasants into starting work hours before dawn.

I bit my lip to stop my tears. My outfit had large flowers, but I wasn't an evil landlord! I couldn't crow like a rooster—I didn't even like roosters. Tears rolled down my cheeks. The crowd didn't quiet down until the bell rang.

Through the morning, we studied four different subjects: Chinese writing, Chinese history, math, and drawing. During recess no one talked to me. Sitting by myself, I stared at the whitewashed wall where a huge portrait of Mao hung above the blackboard. I wondered what I had done wrong.

Laughter and the noise of dribbling basketballs came through the windows. Why were they so happy? How stupid I was to look forward to this all summer. How was I going to survive the rest of the school year?

I couldn't wait to tell Mother when I went home for lunch. Last year, a boy stepped on my new shoes. Mother talked to his parents, and the boy said he was sorry and stopped bothering me.

After morning classes, I raced home and told Mother about the mean kids. "Could you talk to their parents?"

Mother frowned and said impatiently, "Don't wear that dress to school again."

That afternoon, before going back to school, I changed into a white blouse and blue pants, hoping no one would pick on me. But as soon as I walked into the classroom, the short-haired girl, Yu, shrieked, "The little landlord is pretending to be working class."

She shook her dirty finger at me. "We revolutionaries can smell a wolf under her human skin."

"Wolf, wolf, wolf!" her friends chanted.

I glared at her clothes, dirty and covered with patches. "I would rather be a wolf than look like you," I whispered, and walked toward my seat.

The rabbit-faced boy sniffed at me as I passed. Others laughed and made sniffing sounds. My back was instantly soaked with sweat. My knees trembled under my desk until class started. Why were they picking on me for no reason?

The teasing did not stop until the math teacher entered the classroom. He was a stern old man with thick glasses. For the first time, I wished that math class would never end. During breaks, I stayed in my seat and pretended to read Mao's little red book. Fortunately, Yu led everyone outside to bully someone else.

Later, I learned the rabbit-faced boy's name was Gao. His father was an important person sent by the army to oversee the Cultural Revolution in our district.

Yu and Gao continued to bully me by calling me bloodsucking landlord. In less than a week, everyone in the class had stopped using my real name during recess. I did my best to ignore them. If I had only known, I would never have skipped a grade.

One morning in mid-September, I didn't see Father at breakfast.

"Where's Daddy?" I asked Mother.

She set out a glass of homemade soy milk and a plate with two steamed buns and slices of vegetarian sausage. "He went to check on one of his patients."

I was about to ask whether I'd see him before I left for school when weeping noises came down the chimney pipe from upstairs. I stopped eating. "Listen. Someone is crying." It was Mrs. Wong! I jumped out of my chair.

"You stay and finish your breakfast. I'll go." Mother ran toward the door. I hardly ever saw her run. "Ladies should walk with grace," she always told me.

I left my breakfast and pressed my ear to the fireplace pipe. The words were hard to understand. I wished I could turn into a little bug and crawl up the pipe to see what was happening there! Finally, Mother returned with tears in her eyes.

"Dr. Wong disappeared last night after Comrade Li called him to his office."

I was too shocked to cry. What happened to Dr. Wong? I hoped my friend Comrade Li would help us find him. He knew so many people, even the policemen.

"Please, Momma, let me go see Mrs. Wong!"

"No, she's too upset right now. Go! You're late for school." Mother hung my schoolbag over my shoulder and pushed me toward the front door.

I didn't hear a thing Teacher Hui said that day. My thoughts were as busy as the traffic on Victory Road. I wished I could ask Teacher Hui my questions. What happened to Dr. Wong? Did it have to do with his brother in Hong Kong? Was it because he was Dr. Smith's student? If so, what might happen to Father?

That night Father and I met Comrade Li in the hallway coming out of the bathroom.

"Good evening, Comrade Li," said Father. "Could you please tell me what happened to Dr. Wong?"

Comrade Li rudely pushed his way between us. "Dr. Wong is an enemy of the state. He dared to write a letter that criticized Chairman Mao," he said loudly. "That is all you need to know." He slammed his door behind him.

I was shocked that he called Dr. Wong an enemy. Why would he criticize Chairman Mao? Was Comrade Li angry with Father because he was Dr. Wong's best friend?

Father and Mother stayed up late that night, whispering in their bedroom. In my bed, I held Bao-bao tight. My fear for Dr. Wong and Father tore at me like rats tearing at a rice sack.

Will Butterflies Land on Me?

In the following weeks, I spent as much time as I could near the fireplace, listening. Mrs. Wong cried a lot. I didn't hear any sound from Niu. I pictured him hiding in his room like he did when his fish died.

I wanted to be with them, but Mother didn't allow me to go anymore. I knew she visited them late at night when Comrade Li was not home. I saw Mother pack our bamboo basket with food, medicine, and clean clothes. The next day, the basket was empty. One night, when Mother was packing the basket, I slipped out of bed. While Mother was in the kitchen, I hid Bao-bao under a package of herbal medicine. I hoped Bao-bao would help Mrs. Wong sleep at night and comfort her during the day.

Coming home from school a few days later, I saw Comrade Li standing in front of our apartment building with a loudspeaker in his hand. With a wide blue belt over his Mao uniform, he looked taller and skinnier. I ducked behind the trunk of a milk tree and stared.

Young people in Mao uniforms ran in and out of our building. On their right arms they wore red armbands that said RED GUARD in yellow characters. Two carried Mrs. Wong's sewing machine. Four others had her refrigerator. Her airplane heater was smashed into pieces near the stairs. Neighbors peeked out from behind their curtains.

Comrade Li's voice boomed around the courtyard through the loudspeaker. "We confiscate these bourgeois items in the name of the Cultural Revolution."

How could this be the same funny man who did magic tricks for me and sang in the bathroom? I took a deep breath and ran upstairs. To my surprise, Mother sat by the dining room table staring at an empty wall. Why wasn't she helping Mrs. Wong? Why didn't she call Father home to protect us? Would the Red Guards take our things next? I was afraid to ask Mother these questions.

That night, I had a horrible dream. Father was taken away by a mob without faces. I woke up and ran toward my parents' bedroom. I found Father sitting in the living room with a heavy cotton blanket tented over himself and the radio that sat on the round end table. The yellow light from the small lamp cast his shadow on the wall. All I could hear was a humming like tiny mosquitoes.

Father had told me the government jammed foreign stations, because Chairman Mao wanted us to listen only to the Central China People's Broadcast from Beijing. It played Jiang Qing's propaganda songs and repeated Mao's speeches over and over.

"Daddy! What are you listening to?" I whispered.

Father turned off the radio and lifted up a corner of the blanket. His shadow on the wall turned into a sitting Buddha.

"The Voice of America," he whispered.

These days, we had to whisper a lot, especially when we talked about the Golden Gate Bridge, listened to the Voice of America, or held English lessons. I crawled onto his lap and snuggled with him under the blanket. It was warm and smelled of antiseptics.

"Daddy, why do people want to go to America?" I lifted off the blanket.

"Shh!" Father put a finger to his lips.

We glanced toward Comrade Li's apartment. Since Father had asked about Dr. Wong, Comrade Li no longer knocked on the little door. He ignored me when we met in the hallway. It was as if a bad magic trick had changed him from a funny monkey into a poisonous snake.

"They want to enjoy freedom," Father whispered.

"What's freedom?" I whispered back.

Father led me to my bedroom. "Freedom is being able to read what you want and say what you think."

I saw sadness in his eyes. I wanted to ask him if people disappeared in America, but I didn't. Talking about Dr. Wong made Father unhappy.

"For tomorrow's lesson, can we talk about what they eat in America?" I slid under my soft silk blanket.

"All right. Go to sleep now." Father kissed my forehead.

Mother brought home less and less food. On Communist National Day, October 1, she returned with an empty basket. With her tired voice, she said to Father, "Everyone is too busy taking part in the Cultural Revolution." Father put a finger to his lips and looked in the direction of Comrade Li's home. Mother lowered her voice to a whisper. "From now on, everything is rationed." She pulled out small tickets in different colors from her pocket and explained, "Red is for one jin of meat, blue is for five eggs, and yellow is for two bars of soap."

I looked at those colorful tickets and wished they would turn into meat and eggs right then.

That Sunday, Mother and I went to the store to buy meat with a red ticket.

"We're out of meat," said the saleswoman. "Come back in three days."

Although the store shelves were empty, people still waited outside in long lines. That day we ate only rice, shriveled vegetables, and some dried meat.

When the weather grew cooler and leaves fell off

the trees, mealtime had become a passing game. It started when Mother said she was not hungry. She would pass her portion of meat or egg to me and Father. Father would pass them back to her. In the end, it all wound up in my bowl. I didn't understand how Mother could not be hungry. I was hungry all the time.

The week before my tenth birthday, I asked Mother, "When are we going to buy cloth for my outfit?"

In the past, I always got new clothes for my birthday. Mother said it was important so evil spirits would not recognize me in the coming year. For dinner, she would serve me ten dumplings for good luck. I dreamed of eating her plump pork-cabbage dumplings with ginger-sesame sauce. I could almost taste their delicious juice in my mouth.

Since we could rarely buy meat, I could only hope to have a new outfit. I hadn't worn clothes with bright flowers to school, but I still loved to wear them at home. They reminded me of the happy days.

Mother stopped eating and glanced at Father. She put down her chopsticks and said slowly, "Ling, fabric is rationed now. We must save all our ration tickets for winter clothes."

Tears rolled down my cheeks. I couldn't squeeze into last year's clothes. Without a new outfit, butterflies were not going to land on me. Mother closed her eyes and took a deep breath.

Father put down his rice bowl. He gently stroked my hair and said to Mother, "I don't need new clothes this winter. Use my ration ticket to buy fabric for Ling."

Mother shook her head. "You always spoil her." With her ivory chopsticks, Mother reached over to the pan-fried fish in front of me, picked up a large piece, and pressed it firmly in my rice bowl. I was happy she gave me another piece of fish, but wished she would stop treating me like a baby. If I was old enough to braid my hair, I was surely old enough to feed myself.

I didn't feel good about using Father's ration ticket, but I hadn't had a new outfit in so long.

Last year, the fabric store had at least thirty flower prints on the shelves. After two hours, I still hadn't decided whether to get the small white lotus flowers with green leaves or the big bunches of yellow chrysanthemums in gold and blue vases. Father had suggested I get both fabrics, the lotus for a blouse and the chrysanthemums for a skirt.

Mother and I took the fabric to Mrs. Wong's home. She made me the skirt and blouse on her beautiful sewing machine.

With the leftover fabric, Mrs. Wong made me a sun hat. When Father saw me in my new outfit, he told me that I would mix right in with the chrysanthemums in our courtyard. They were the last to bloom before winter came. A few times, the big black and golden butterflies had even landed on me.

Whenever I wore the outfit to Father's office, the young nurses surrounded me. "What a beautiful little flower." They stuffed my pocket with candy and sweet dried plums. I enjoyed the attention and treats, but I didn't like it when they pinched my cheeks.

Now that outfit was too small.

Mother met me after school. As we walked to the Number One Fabric Store, I felt happier than I had in a long time. I told Mother, "The butterflies only landed on me five times last year. I think the flowers were too small. I'll try to find bigger ones this year." Even though I couldn't wear my new outfit to school, I could put it on at home or when I went out with Father.

When we entered the fabric store, most of the shelves were empty. The only fabric color for sale was dark blue.

"Do you want to buy fabric for a Mao uniform?" asked a tall woman behind the counter. Her face looked like a dried-up eggplant. She yanked out some blue fabric wrapped around a long board and spread it open on the wooden counter, the same fabric her jacket was made of.

"No. I want flowered fabric," I whispered. Mother squeezed my arm but it was too late.

The woman raised her voice to a high pitch. "Flowered fabric?" Other people in the store stared at us. She waved around her bony hands. "That is bourgeois! We are a revolutionary store. We don't sell idiotic flowered fabrics!"

Mother grabbed my hand and dragged me out of the store. Clerks laughed loudly behind us.

On the way home, Mother was quiet. Crowds of people all dressed in dark clothes pushed past us on the sidewalk, bumping into my shoulders. I gathered my courage and asked her in a small voice, "Momma, what's bourgeois? Why are flower fabrics bourgeois?"

She grabbed my hand and stopped under a big Chairman Mao poster, a terrified look on her face. "Please stop your questions!"

I whispered back, "But why?"

"Because I don't have any answers." She let go of my hand and started walking.

From the poster, Mao's picture smiled down at me, as always. We were told every day that he loved us and was our savior. Would he help me to get a flower outfit for my birthday?

I heard cheers and screams as we came to our courtyard. Inside, the Red Guards who had robbed Mrs. Wong's home were back. Their dirty faces were smeared with soy sauce. They sang in celebration as they tore up and stomped on the flowers Gardener Zong had planted. A few black and yellow butterflies hovered over the destroyed flowers and broken branches. Gardener Zong squatted in front of his single-room apartment. With his elbows on his knees, his hands covered the back of his head. When we walked by, he didn't look up.

The next day, Father whispered to Mother that two more doctors from his department had disappeared.

The Terrifying Birthday

Each day, my list of questions grew. But I had no one to ask. Father no longer told me, "Smart children always ask questions." Instead, now he said, "Children don't have to know everything."

The air around the city was heavy with the smell of ink and molding paste. Everything was covered with layers of Mao's pictures and teachings. Loudspeakers blasted out the same songs day and night, like a thousand crows following me around.

> *The East is red, the sun has risen.*
> *China has produced Mao Zedong!*
> *He works for the people's happiness,*
> *He is the people's savior.*

I couldn't think of one happy thing that he had brought me. But I knew better than to say this to anyone. Mother told me about an eight-year-old boy who had been reported to the police because he told someone that "'Revolution' means being hungry." His parents, who were doctors, were accused of teaching their son antirevolutionary thoughts. Three days later, the whole family was sent to a labor camp.

I stopped to greet the neighbors when I met them. Mother used to tell me that a well-mannered child should always greet elders with respect, like "good morning, Aunt or Uncle." But lately, when I greeted them, they either pretended they didn't hear me or looked at me as if I was a stranger. Neighbors no longer chatted in the courtyard or visited in front of the buildings after dinner.

At school, Gao and Yu were happy to tell anyone willing to listen that I was from a nonworking, bourgeois family. I told them my parents worked every day in the hospital, but no one listened. They said only parents who worked in a factory, in the army, or on a farm were working class.

After hearing I was from a bourgeois family, even my old friends stopped talking to me. When Hong and I met in school, she glanced away. When I tried to talk to her, she whispered, "I don't want to be called a bourgeois sympathizer," and ran away.

At times I wished my family was poor and my parents worked on a vegetable farm like Yu's, so I could have friends. But if my parents worked on a farm, who would treat their patients?

Yu often complained that she got to wear only clothes handed down from her six older sisters. Perhaps my clothes had no patches because my father was happy to have just one daughter. I didn't have to wear hand-me-downs.

I wished her family had stopped at daughter number six. Then there would be no Yu to pick on me. Even though I didn't have friends, I was glad I was not Yu. With seven daughters, her father must have never had time to talk to her.

In the morning before I left for school, Mother always reminded me, "No germs can get into a closed mouth." I wanted to tell her not to worry, that I hardly talked at school since I had no friends. But I was too ashamed to say that.

Although I had the highest test scores in math and writing, no one nominated me for the Young Pioneers.

I was one of the few students in my class who didn't have a red scarf. I hated school.

On the afternoon of October 29, my tenth birthday, I jumped out of my seat when I saw Father standing outside my classroom.

"Where are we going today, Daddy?" I ran to him and grabbed his hand.

"We're going home." He didn't pat my shoulder as he usually did.

Father sometimes picked me up before afternoon school ended. I was always happy to see him, especially when I didn't have to sit through the daily history class and recite the endless dates and names of battles Chairman Mao had won.

The year before, whenever Father picked me up, we rode bus number 7 three stops to our favorite Western pastry shop, Hing Shing. The clerk would greet us warmly as we entered the red wooden doors. She was a cheerful, middle-aged lady in a white uniform. The small store had a high glass counter that held dark chocolate cakes and all kinds of desserts, including my favorite cow-horn–shaped pastries. Since Mother said Father should get some rest after performing surgeries instead of taking me places, we kept our outings a secret. Our special code was "Let's go get poked by the cow's horn."

Father and I would sit at one of the three little round tables outside Hing Shing, eating, chatting, and sipping coffee while watching people, bicycles, and buses pass by. We had so much to say to each other. I didn't care for the bitter coffee, but I took tiny sips like Father. Educated people drank coffee, and I wanted to be one when I grew up. The cow-horn pastry was coated with big grains of sugar and filled with fluffy cream. Father said I was very skillful at eating pastry. First I licked the sugar off the outside. Then I sank my teeth into the sweet cream inside, savoring each bite. When I couldn't reach the cream anymore, I nibbled away at the shell over my cup. The butter from the crumbs would float to the surface. At last, I sipped the coffee from a small sugar spoon, like Father. Now it tasted sweet and less bitter. Before we left the store, we had the friendly clerk pack an extra cow horn in a small box for Mother. When Mother asked where it came from, we would tell her it was given to us by a passing cow.

The last time we had gone to Hing Shing, someone had sealed off the doors with long strips of red paper that read BOURGEOIS NEST.

Today, I had hoped we would do something special for my birthday. "Can we go to the Han River?" That was our new favorite place. Sitting on its bank, we counted boats and practiced our English. Since few people went there during the day, we felt safe talking.

"Not today." Father took hold of my hand. I had to take big steps to keep up with him. The air was cool and wet. It smelled of burning paper. A few small drops of rain fell on my face. The sun tried to peek from behind dark clouds.

I wanted to ask why, but the serious look on his face stopped me.

Inside our courtyard, Comrade Li and the Red Guards were pasting new posters and slogans on tree trunks and all three buildings. The air was heavy with the smell of fresh ink. I spotted a white poster with Father's name on it in black ink. Over his name was a big blood-red X.

"Why are they doing this, Daddy?" I whispered. Father held my hand tighter and walked faster without answering. Once in our apartment, he ran to the fire-place, lit a fire, and threw in his letters and books. Wisps of burned paper bumped around inside the fire-place like frightened black butterflies. He even threw in his red tie and the English book we had made together. The fire slowly destroyed the picture of the little girl—first her dress, then her ice cream, and finally her face and hair. Sitting in Father's large leather chair, I fought back tears, feeling my happy days were burning away with the girl.

Father picked up the picture of the Golden Gate Bridge from above the fireplace. I held my breath as he stared at it. At last, he put it back. "I can't do it. Not yet," he mumbled. I let out my breath.

I had thought Comrade Li was my friend. I always gave him what he wanted to buy. Why was he doing all these bad things to us now? I should never have played the buying and selling game with him. I ran to my room and carried out the basket full of origami. When Father went to get more books to burn, I dumped all of Comrade Li's origami into the fire.

Mother dashed in. She and Father went into the kitchen, whispering. I heard Father say "Mrs. Wong?"

and parts of Mother's answer: "Red Guard . . . labor camp. . . ."

What were they going to do to Mrs. Wong this time? I wished a fairy could fly through their French doors and carry her and Niu away.

Sucking in my lower lip, I peeked through the kitchen door. Mother stuffed herbal medicine bottles and rice cakes into a cloth rice sack. Father stood next to the window, watching the courtyard.

In a low, serious voice, Father said, "Be careful. Come back soon."

Mother nodded and ran out the door with the brown bag.

A few moments later, yelling came from the courtyard. Father ran to the fireplace and banged loudly with his knuckles on the chimney pipe.

My heart drummed. The crowd shouted, "Long live Chairman Mao! Long live the Cultural Revolution!" I tried to shut out the chants by putting my hands over my ears. But I could still hear "Red Guard . . . Build the new China. . . ."

Many feet drummed up the stairs. Mother dashed back into our apartment. In her arm, she held Bao-bao.

Father locked the door behind her. She couldn't speak. Her face was pale, and she gasped for breath. I took Bao-bao from her. The doll had on a new dress over the old outfit. It was made from the fabric with the little girls in red sun hats sitting on the beach. I held her tight against my face. Bao-bao smelled of jasmine tea, like Mrs. Wong. My eyes swelled with tears. From upstairs came the sounds of people shouting, furniture crashing, shrieking laughter, and dishes breaking. Sobbing came down the chimney. It was from both Mrs. Wong and Niu.

Father held us in his arms, in front of the fireplace, under the picture of the Golden Gate Bridge. Buzzing noises filled my ears, as if a thousand flies had crowded into my head. My body trembled. I stared at the picture, wishing we could hide inside the clouds around the bridge. Some time went by and then, "Everybody!" Comrade Li squawked through his loudspeaker. "Report to the courtyard!"

Father patted my shoulder. "Ling, we have to go downstairs. It will be all right."

Mother took Bao-bao from my arms and set her on Father's chair. "Leave it here." I clung to Father's arm as we slowly went down the stairs. The autumn sun had disappeared behind the dark clouds. The milk trees had shed their blossoms, but there was still a touch of sweet scent in the air. Fallen leaves carpeted the courtyard. When the cold wind blew, bright yellow leaves rained down, like the tears in my heart. Ravens cawed from the high wall surrounding the courtyard. The Red Guards had pulled old tables out of the first-floor storage room and set up a small stage. Doctors and nurses from the two neighboring buildings gathered around.

One teenage boy, face covered with pimples, shoved Mrs. Wong and Niu onto the stage. Five more Red Guards stood around the stage, jeering. Mrs. Wong's silk skirt was torn in the front. She held it together with both hands. Her long hair fell over her face.

Niu's face was white. He kept pushing up his glasses. Behind them his eyes darted around and stopped when he saw our family. Our eyes met, and I saw his fear and sadness. I wished his father was here to protect him or that we could save them. Father held my hand. Mother stood next to us, shivering.

Through his loudspeaker, Comrade Li sounded like an angry goose. "Dr. Wong is an American spy! Mrs. Wong is an example of the bourgeois!"

I thought *bourgeois* meant "evil things from the old days." But Mrs. Wong wasn't old and evil. She was the nicest person I knew. How could she be an example of the bourgeois?

One girl with short straight hair and plump pink cheeks waved a pair of scissors in the air. She pointed them at Mrs. Wong's hair and shouted, "Look at the symbol of the bourgeoisie. Let's get rid of the old!"

Her friends cheered.

Pink Cheeks climbed onto the table and thrust the scissors at Mrs. Wong. "Cut your bourgeois hair."

Mrs. Wong raised her head. Her eyes were fixed on the distance, as if her mind had been taken away by the ravens. Her hands still clung to her torn skirt.

The loudspeaker squealed as Comrade Li shouted, "Let's do a revolutionary deed!" He stood at the left corner of the stage, his army cap askew on his head, the visor almost covering his left eye. His blue jacket was buttoned all the way up. The crowd of young people cheered again.

My teeth clicked. Father held my hand tighter. I felt a knot in my throat. My eyes blurred with tears.

I wanted to hide under the milk tree leaves.

Pink Cheeks raised the scissors.

I closed my eyes.

Another wave of cheers.

My hand hurt from Father's tight grip. I forced my eyes open. A lock of Mrs. Wong's long, dark hair floated off the table and formed a question mark on the bright yellow leaves.

I was too afraid to cry aloud; my heart wept silently.

Tears flowed down Mrs. Wong's face.

"You!" Pink Cheeks pushed Niu. He almost fell off the table. "Turn against your bourgeois parents! Follow our leader, Chairman Mao!" she shouted.

Niu closed his eyes.

Pimple Face, barely taller than Niu, climbed on stage. He shouted, "We are the Red Guards, devoted followers of our great leader, Chairman Mao. Let's destroy the old system and build a new China!"

Other Red Guards repeated after him, "Long live our great leader, Chairman Mao!"

Comrade Li's mouth twisted, and a wicked smile

broke out on his face. He handed Pimple Face a heavy rectangular blackboard. Harshly pushing Mrs. Wong's head down, Pimple Face threw the loop of rope attached to the board over her neck. Mrs. Wong fell to her knees. I wanted to turn into a powerful dragon, burn the Red Guards and Comrade Li with flames shooting from my mouth. Then I would carry her away.

Comrade Li pointed at each word on the board as he barked, "Symbol of the bourgeoisie."

Father passed my hand to Mother. I held on tight to her ice-cold fingers. She tightened her hold on mine.

Straightening his broad shoulders, holding his head high, Father shouted to the crowd, "Let me through!"

I tried to call him back, but I couldn't make any sound. It felt like the time when a fish bone was caught in my throat. I pressed half my face into Mother's sleeve.

Silence fell. People moved back to give him room. All eyes followed him as he moved to the front and stopped between Mrs. Wong and the crowd. I noticed a hole at the elbow of his gray wool sweater.

Mother shook so hard I had to let go of her hand. I bit my lower lip so my teeth wouldn't chatter. Father took the board off Mrs. Wong's neck and threw it on the ground.

"I have known Dr. Wong and Mrs. Wong for fifteen years." Father's voice was stern. "They could have moved overseas years ago, but they chose to stay and help build a better China." He glared at Comrade Li. "They've done nothing wrong!"

Some people in the crowd nodded. Others whispered. A couple of young doctors from Father's department came up. They helped Mrs. Wong to her feet and supported her back to her home. Comrade Li and his Red Guards gathered around the stage. They stared at Father when he lifted Niu off the stage. Niu hurried past Mother and me without looking at us. The crowd broke up, except for Comrade Li and his group of Red Guards.

That night I climbed into Father's lap in his big chair. The warmth of his shoulder and his familiar smell made me feel safe and protected. Now he was not only a great father but also a hero. On my birthday, he had saved Mrs. Wong.

Crushed under the Heel

As the first week of November passed, the weather in Wuhan changed quickly. Days of chilly rain turned to snow. Our apartment was cold and damp. I moved around feeling like a miserable panda in my heavy cotton outfit. At night, Mother piled three heavy quilts on me.

On the afternoon of December 14, I returned from school and found Niu sitting in our living room crying. Mother told me they had taken Mrs. Wong to a labor camp. Tears streamed down my cheeks. Never had I felt so heartbroken. I hadn't seen Mrs. Wong since that awful day. She hadn't come down, and Mother didn't allow me to go up when she went. I wished I had had a chance to say good-bye to Mrs. Wong and thank her for Bao-bao's new outfit.

Despite my parents insisting Niu move in with us, he went home every night. But he spent a lot of time at our apartment during the day. He talked to me only when I asked him a question. Trying to cheer him up, I showed him my special collections: a cotton scarf with various Mao buttons pinned on it, a folder filled with plastic candy wrappers, and a small chocolate box that held my treasured pair of silk ribbons, a phoenix-shaped plastic darning needle, and a carved sandalwood fan. He only glanced at them and his sullen face didn't change. I wasn't sure how to make him feel better.

Over the following months, more doctors were forced to leave the hospital. Some were sent to jail or labor camps. Others just disappeared, like Dr. Wong. I wished someone could assure me that Father would be safe. I became so afraid of my nightmares that I tried to stay awake as long as I could.

Lately after dinner Father would either read his medical journals or stare at the picture of the Golden Gate Bridge. I thought that if only he would spend more time telling stories about the bridge and America, I might have a happy dream.

*   *   *

The week before Chinese New Year, Comrade Li pasted a new poster on the side of our building.

With your blood and sweat,
wash away your antirevolutionary sins!

When I passed it, I turned my head away from the red characters. The word *blood* made me shiver.

That night, Father stroked my cheek gently. "Wake up, Ling. You're having a bad dream."

"Daddy, don't let them cut my hair!" I reached up to make sure both my braids were still there and held them tightly under my chin.

In my dream, a group of faceless people surrounded me, waving scissors. I tried to hide my hair in my hat, but my braids were too long and kept falling out.

Father tucked me snugly under the blanket. "Ling, I promise I won't let anyone cut your hair." Feeling safe with him sitting next to my bed, I drifted back to sleep.

The next morning, a loud sound woke me.

"What's happening, Daddy?" I called out.

"Nothing to worry about." Father's low voice came from the living room. "Go back to sleep."

Smelling burned paper, I ran out of my bedroom and saw Father throw a stack of pictures into the fireplace. The flames swallowed them like hungry monsters. Photo albums lay on the floor.

Mother stood next to the window. "Hurry! Hurry! They've finished their morning march."

Trembling, I lifted a photo of Father in a Western suit. He stood before a palm tree. Next to him was Dr. Smith, an older man with brown hair, also in a suit. Both looked handsome. "Do you have to burn this?" I asked in a low voice. Father glanced at the picture, and tossed another handful of photographs into the fire, among them two photos of my dead grandparents. Father used to keep them on his desk.

"We can't keep any old photos now. They are considered evil reminders of the bourgeois lifestyle."

"But I'll forget what my grandparents looked like—"

Someone pounded on our door. "Open! Open up."

Mother's face turned white. Father rose and rushed toward the door. In his hurry, he knocked over a chair next to the table. I tucked the picture of Father and Dr. Smith into the elastic of my pants.

Five Red Guards burst into our home. I recognized Pimple Face and Pink Cheeks. Comrade Li followed. Their rubber army boots stepped on the open photo albums, leaving yellow-brown marks on the pictures. Mother and I backed into the corner next to the fireplace. Father came and stood in front of us.

Once in the middle of our living room, Comrade Li lifted up his arm and yelled, "One! Two!"

The Red Guards quickly lined up facing Chairman Mao's portrait above the fireplace. My heart pounded.

"Start!" He swung down his hand.

There's a golden sun in Beijing.

They sang and waved their hands above their heads and made a turn.

It brightens whatever it shines upon.

Goose bumps covered my forearms.

The light doesn't come from the sky but from
Our great leader Chairman Mao.

They swung their legs, bent at their waists, and stretched their arms above their heads.

"Long live Chairman Mao!" yelled Comrade Li.

"Down with the bourgeois!" shouted the Red Guards.

As if chased by lightning, they darted in different directions. Pink Cheeks pasted a long white strip of paper onto our living room wall. In ugly chicken-scratch letters it read BOURGEOIS SYMPATHIZERS.

Pimple Face dumped a plastic bottle of alcohol into our fireplace. The flames leaped out as if trying to grab us. Comrade Li pulled Father's books from the shelves and threw them into the fire.

Another Red Guard boy with short legs put his head and hands on the ground, kicked his feet up, and spun around. The group cheered.

Pink Cheeks twirled Mother's pearl necklace around in the air. I closed my eyes, only to force them open when I heard clattering. She had flung the necklace across the room and it hit the wall, sending loose pearls everywhere.

Mother buried her face in Father's shoulder. Father wrapped his arms around me. I wished I could turn into a little rabbit and hide inside his coat.

Waving a big cleaver above his head, the Red Guard with paintbrush eyebrows slashed a ragged X into the back of Father's chair. White stuffing burst out. Feeling the strength of Father's arm and the warmth of his body, I again imagined becoming a dragon and gobbling them up.

Why did Comrade Li bring these Red Guards to our home? Did he want to chase us out so he could have our entire apartment to himself? Had he found out we were hiding coffee and chocolate from him? Or was he angry with us for being friends with the Wongs?

Pink Cheeks and another Red Guard girl with mouse eyes stomped into my bedroom.

Please, please don't take my Bao-bao, I prayed.

Father whispered, "Be strong, my dear."

I held my breath. Cackles came from my bedroom. I wanted to run inside to save Bao-bao, but my legs would not move.

Trotting into the living room, Pink Cheeks dangled Bao-bao by a leg. "Look at this silly little thing."

"Oh, it even has a dress on," said Mouse Eyes. "Let me see what's under here." She ripped up Bao-bao's new dress with the girl in the sun hat.

Anger filled my chest. I let go of Father and ran to them. "Leave her alone. She's mine!" I grabbed one of Bao-bao's arms.

Pink Cheeks jerked back. The arm came off with an awful ripping sound.

I dropped it to the floor and couldn't bear to look.

The Red Guards roared with laughter.

Grabbing a heavy photo album from the floor, I threw it at them. "I hate you!" I screamed.

Silence filled the room. Father grabbed me and hugged me tight.

With a big grin, Comrade Li stepped forward and said, "Dear comrades, when the enemy hates us, that's when we are doing a good job. Work harder!" He waved his hand.

When had we become his enemies? What had we done?

Mouse Eyes picked up Bao-bao and her arm and threw them into the fireplace.

"Oh, no!" cried Mother.

I couldn't bear to watch the fire swallow Bao-bao. *Bao-bao, I am sorry I couldn't protect you.* I buried my face in Father's sleeve and squeezed his arm tightly. I didn't want the Red Guards to see me sobbing.

Thud! Crash! Another wave of cheers and shouts filled our home. Paintbrush had knocked the picture of the Golden Gate Bridge off the mantel with his cleaver. Short Legs had swept the blue vase onto the floor with a broomstick. Jumping behind Father to avoid the flying pieces, I thought of the powerful dragon that could spit fire. I wanted to burn them to ashes.

Father pulled away from me and stepped in front of Comrade Li.

"We're on a revolutionary mission. No time to talk." Comrade Li shoved him aside and walked into our kitchen.

Father's face trembled. I realized he could not protect us.

Mouse Eyes lifted our radio up above her head as Comrade Li walked out of our kitchen, holding a bag of rice and eating a banana. He motioned her to stop, but it was too late. She smashed it on the floor. The black plastic box cracked open, showing tubes and wires.

Stuffing the last bite of banana into his mouth, he mumbled, "Stupid! I could have used it to further the Revolution."

Comrade Li turned to Father. "Listen! If you dare to say or do anything more against the Revolution . . ." Dropping the banana peel in front of Father, he mashed it under his boot, turned, and marched out the door. Pimple Face, Short Legs, Mouse Eyes, and Paintbrush followed, with their arms full of our clothes, dishes, and food. Clutching the chocolate box filled with my treasures, Pink Cheeks slammed the door. A shred of Bao-bao's dress hung on the door latch. My tears rolled out in despair.

Father picked up the picture of the Golden Gate Bridge. The heavy gold frame had protected it. He held it close to his heart and sat down in his torn-up chair. It was the first time I ever saw tears in his eyes.

Tears trickled down Mother's cheeks as she righted the remaining chairs. Two of them were now missing arms. My flower comforter lay across the floor, torn in half. Around us, scattered pearls mixed with mud, silk rags, broken glass, and torn pages.

Was Comrade Li going to crush us like he did the banana peel? Did Chairman Mao order him to do this? If so, why were we told Chairman Mao was our savior?

I pulled the picture out from the elastic band of my pants. It was warm from being against my body. I handed it to Father. His eyes brightened.

"Remember, my dear, in America people believe in justice." His voice dropped to a whisper. "One day we will go there."

I had always believed Father could make good things happen, but how could that be possible? No one was allowed to even leave the city.

PART TWO

BAMBOO IN THE WIND

Spring 1974 – Winter 1976

Revolution Is Not a Dinner Party

It took us over a week to clean up the mess left by the Red Guards' raid. Mother and I gathered and folded the linen and clothes that weren't torn. She put aside a small pile that needed mending and another larger pile for rags. Among the rags were her white silk dress and Father's silk ties.

Cleaning the kitchen took the longest. Black sesame seeds, red beans, and dry spices were scattered everywhere. Broken dishes filled the sink. Mother's face was blank until she picked up a piece of her fine china. Then she burst into tears.

I felt like crying again, too, but I didn't want Mother to see. I joined Father and Niu in the living room. Father glued broken legs on chairs, and Niu wrapped them with bandages and tape. When they finished, all our chair legs wore casts.

In the following days, Father and Niu spent hours repairing the radio. When they finally got it working, they left the back open, but it still looked broken.

Mother hid the picture of the Golden Gate Bridge behind the large portrait of Chairman Mao above the fireplace. We pasted small Mao portraits in every room.

"Why are we putting up so many?" I brushed rice glue on the back of a small portrait.

"It's like the incense we burn in the summer to keep the mosquitoes away." Mother took the portrait from me and carried it into her bedroom.

Father covered a piece of Chinese calligraphy with Chairman Mao's teaching about the class struggle. In my reading class at school, we were required to study it until we could write the whole passage from memory.

A revolution is not a dinner party, or writing an essay, or painting a picture, or doing embroidery; it cannot be so refined, so leisurely and gentle, so temperate, kind, courteous, restrained, and magnanimous. A revolution is an insurrection, an act of violence by which one class overthrows another.

I didn't understand what "class" and "revolution" had to do with a dinner party. How I wished Mrs. Wong and Dr. Wong would come back and we could have a big dinner party so Niu would smile again. I missed all the dishes Mother used to make, even her strange ones.

The calligraphy Father was hiding was written on blue rice paper in small ink characters. It had been under the glass top of Father's desk for as long as I could remember. He used to tell the young doctors who came to visit that it was the best guidance for anyone who wanted to be a doctor.

During last summer vacation, I memorized every word, even though I didn't really understand their meaning. Father was impressed when I recited it to him.

Physician's Creed

Whenever a great physician treats diseases, he has to be mentally calm and his disposition firm. He should not give way to wishes and desires but must first develop a marked attitude of compassion. He should commit himself firmly to a willingness to make an effort to save every living creature.

*A great physician should not pay attention to
status, wealth, or age. Nor should he question
whether his patient is an enemy or friend. . . . He
should meet everyone on equal ground; he should
always act as if he were thinking of himself; he is
not to ponder over his own fortune or misfortune and
should thus preserve life and have compassion for it.*

*Whoever acts in this manner is a great physician
for the living. Whoever acts contrary to these
commands is a great thief of those who still have
their spirits.*

After the last Red Guard raid, Father was ordered to
mop floors and scrub bathrooms in the hospital. He
could no longer work as a doctor.

Instead of treating patients with herbal medicines,
Mother had to work nights as a nurse in the emergency room. I didn't know how she got any sleep. All
day long, loudspeakers outside our apartment shouted
out Chairman Mao's teachings, played revolutionary
songs, and announced the names of people accused
of being counterrevolutionaries. My breath short-
ened whenever I heard Father's name.

Despite all this, Father told us we should look for joy even during hard times. The nights when the electricity to our building was cut off and Comrade Li was not home, Father closed the windows and lit a small candle. He taught me how to dance the two-step and the waltz. I was quick to learn.

I asked Father to teach me the tango, but he said our living room was too small to practice. When Father and Mother used to tango at parties, everyone had stopped to watch. Mother wore her long white silk dress. As she gracefully swung out her leg, I could see her shiny silver high heels.

"They can't keep people from dancing forever. Someday I will teach you at a dance hall." Father made a graceful turn with one hand spread out and the other resting on his hip.

I dreamt of wearing a red silk dress and dancing with a handsome young surgeon. Niu didn't want to practice with me after he stepped on my shoes a few times.

I was sad he had lost both his parents and had no one at home to take care of him. But in my heart, I had to admit that I wished he wasn't spending so much time with us, taking my parents' attention away from me. During our English lessons, he loved to show off, acting as if he already knew every new word. I missed those times when Father taught only me.

One good thing about having the lessons with Niu was that he suggested Father teach us English folk songs, since now we had only one English book left, a small dictionary. Father had hidden it in his boot before the Red Guards' raid.

After school, when we were sure Comrade Li wasn't home and my parents were still at work, Niu and I hid under the heavy cotton blanket, like Father did at night, and searched the dial for English stations. When we found one playing folk songs we knew, he tapped his left foot and wiggled his head as he sang along. Occasionally, he'd scrunch up his nose to nudge his glasses into place. I was happy to see a smile on his face. In less than a week, I memorized every word of "Row, Row, Row Your Boat." The song filled my heart with happiness. Niu and I hooked our pinkies and promised we would never tell anyone about listening to foreign stations. I thought of Niu even more like a real brother now.

* * *

Mother served us less and less food each day. No longer did she put the best food in my bowl; she now split it between Niu and me. I used to hate tofu and seaweed, but these days I ate every bit Mother offered.

One evening we were just sitting down for dinner when Comrade Li barged in.

"Well, well, Niu fits right in here." He stretched out his neck and coughed over the dishes on the table—a bowl of stir-fried vegetables with small shrimp shells, pan-fried tofu in black bean sauce, and white rice. Anger stirred inside me. Hadn't his mother taught him to cover his mouth when he coughed? With one finger pointed upward, he said, "Niu, go upstairs and get your clothes. Here is your new home. Don't touch the rest of the stuff. We are taking your apartment for the Revolution." He spat on the floor next to me and turned toward the door.

Father slammed down his chopsticks. Comrade Li spun around at the noise. Before Father could say anything, I stood up and screamed, "You are a poisonous snake! You took away his parents, now *mmphllphmm*—"

Mother had darted out of her chair and reached to cover my mouth all in one fluid motion, as if she had predicted this moment. "Sorry, sorry. She's just a child." Her voice trembled with fear. "We'll go upstairs and help Niu pack."

Comrade Li glared at Father. "Keep your wild girl under control! Or I will teach her a lesson!" He stormed out, leaving our door wide open.

Father sat, face serious and drawn, staring at Chairman Mao's portrait above the fireplace. Was he thinking about how to protect us from Comrade Li or how to find a way to take us to the Golden Gate Bridge—to freedom?

Tears flickered in Niu's eyes. He got up and rushed to the door. Mother and I followed him upstairs. The apartment smelled of sandalwood. Broken dishes, torn clothes, and paper were spread around crippled furniture. Someone had sliced the painting of the French girl with braids pinned around her head. Now her face was cut in half.

In his parents' bedroom, Niu walked over to the red sandalwood chest that stood opposite the bed. I ran my fingers over a carved phoenix. Seeing the curtains on the windows reminded me of Mrs. Wong sitting in front of her sewing machine. The little girls in red sun hats on the curtains were dusty and seemed tired.

In a gloomy voice, Niu said, "Help me." He grabbed one of the brass handles on the side of the chest.

Mother and I took the other one. Together we moved the heavy chest out half an inch from the wall. Niu slid his fingers behind and pulled out a brown envelope.

"What's in there?"

Ignoring my question, he tucked the envelope in the waistband of his pants under his shirt. He then stuffed a small canvas bag on the floor with clothes Mother gathered for him.

Back in our home, Niu took out the envelope. Inside were a map and a sheet of thin paper. It was a letter from his uncle, asking his family to leave China and join him in Hong Kong.

I remembered Dr. Wong had shown Father the letter two days before his disappearance and told him it had been opened before he received it.

One afternoon when I came home from school, Niu quickly covered something on the dinner table as I opened the door. Seeing it was me, he lifted up the newspaper. "Come, let me show you something."

I couldn't remember the last time he had talked so cheerfully. With my schoolbag still in hand, I ran to the table. His map was spread out.

"What's so important about your map?" I wished he would play a game with me.

"It's our only hope." Niu tapped the map with a finger.

"What do you mean?"

"By swimming across this river to Hong Kong." He drew a short line with his finger from Canton, a city in southern China, to a small island.

"Is it dangerous?" I leaned over his torn map. "What happens if you get caught?"

"I don't know. But it's better to take the chance than to stay here. I might be able to take you with me."

He seemed sure I would leave my parents and go with him. How could he think that? Besides, I didn't even know how to swim. Dr. Wong had taught Niu in the narrow Han River. Unlike other kids who learned swimming by floating on plastic basins or old inner tubes, Dr. Wong had bought Niu a bright yellow life ring. At the end of that summer, Niu told me he no longer needed the life ring and I could have it when I was ready to learn. But Mother said a girl didn't need to learn to swim.

"What about the guards? Won't they shoot you?"

"That won't stop me. Swear you won't tell anyone, not even your parents." Niu held out his pinkie and curled it into a hook. I hesitated, then hooked mine around his, sealing the promise.

"See the river here? It's not that wide." Niu pointed at a small green part of the map.

"Where is America?" I asked, hoping to take his mind away from the escape. Picturing him being shot in the water frightened me. "I bet it takes a long time to sail across the Pacific Ocean."

"You don't need to sail. After you get to Hong Kong, you take an airplane." Niu's finger traced across the map from Hong Kong to America. My heart filled with joy just thinking about the Golden Gate Bridge. It felt so good to imagine going to America.

"I would love to go there. Then I could sing and dance." I stood up and made a ballet turn.

Niu interrupted me. "I only want to get away from here!" With my hands still up in the air, I stopped and studied him. He gazed outside the window into the November rain, as if he could see all the way to Hong Kong.

"I wish I knew magic," I whispered and put down my hands.

"Magic won't help." Niu banged his fist on the table. "The only way out is to escape!"

Drawing a Class Line

In less than two months, there were many changes. By the beginning of June, Gao and Yu's gang stood at the school gates each morning. Everyone entering, including the teachers, had to show their "three-piece treasure," a Mao jacket, a Mao button, and Mao's little red book of revolutionary instructions. If anyone forgot, the gang would decide the punishment. When our old math teacher left his button at home, he was ordered to clean the bathrooms for a week. Two boys were ordered to stand at the back of the classroom for a day. I started to wake up at night, worried about forgetting my "three-piece treasure." Several times I'd get up to make sure the little red book was in the inner pocket of my schoolbag.

Now we had class only in the morning. In the afternoon, the Young Pioneers took turns leading reading sessions of Chairman Mao's teachings. Since Father was accused of being a bourgeois sympathizer, I had no chance of ever becoming a Young Pioneer.

After I told Father that I was the only one in the class without the red scarf around my neck, he looked into my eyes and said, "Remember, my dear, Young Pioneer or not, you are always my special, smart girl."

Father's words didn't make me feel better. Then one day during math class I saw Yu wipe strings of green snot off her nose with her red scarf. Days later, she picked at the crusty stain. I decided that I didn't want one anymore. I looked forward to Sundays, when there was no school.

On a rainy December day, Niu brought home a red slip from school.

> It is necessary for intellectual students to go to the countryside and be re-educated by the working class—the peasants.

Niu and the rest of the high school students in Wuhan were ordered to be "re-educated." The radio said, "The peasants' hands are dirty from the field, but their love for Chairman Mao and Communism is pure and strong."

I wondered why people had to get their hands dirty to show their love. I hated to get mine dirty.

Would Niu have to work as hard as those who went to the labor camps, like Mrs. Wong? We still hadn't found out where they had taken Dr. Wong.

That night, Mother and I helped Niu pack. He tried on his winter jacket. The sleeves were two inches short, and he was barely able to button up the front. My parents went into their bedroom. Moments later Father came out carrying his winter coat and his gray wool sweater—his wedding gift from Mother.

"Take these. Be careful what you say." Father handed the sweater and coat to Niu.

Niu pushed Father's hands back. "I can't take these. What would *you* wear for the winter?"

"Don't worry," said Father with a grin. "The last places still heated in the hospital are the surgical rooms. I bet they're going to have me back there soon."

I took the sweater from Father and folded it into a neat square. As I set it on top of a pile of Niu's clothes, I worried that we might not have enough money and ration tickets to buy Father winter clothes. How would Father stay warm if they didn't allow him to be a doctor again?

Mother sighed.

I ran to my room. In the bottom drawer I had hidden a small package. It was tightly wrapped in newspaper. Inside were two chocolate bars in gold and brown plastic wrappers. Holding them to my nose, I took a deep breath. They no longer smelled as rich as when I hid them last year, but I could still imagine the bittersweet chocolate slowly melting and spreading on my tongue. I took one more deep breath and quickly ran to the living room and stuffed them into Niu's bag. Mother gave me her approving smile, which made me feel less sad about giving up the chocolate.

The next morning when I woke, Niu was gone. After school, coming back to our empty home, I realized how much I missed him. He had been my only friend.

We received a letter from Niu a week later. They had sent him to a border town in South China to work on a rubber plantation. Twice a month we received a short letter from him. At the end of summer, the letters stopped, but Father continued writing to him every week.

Could he have forgotten about us? I couldn't bear the thought that something bad might have happened to him. I worried about him every day.

One rainy night, Father sat next to my bed, telling me my favorite tale of how the Monkey King gathered peaches in the forest, when the loudspeaker called for everybody to report to the courtyard. Mother quickly collected our raincoats and helped me get dressed. In the courtyard, Comrade Li was standing on an office chair with a group of Red Guards gathered around him. I recognized Mouse Eyes and Short Legs. Neighbors stood whispering in small groups under brown oilpaper umbrellas. Rumbling thunder followed slashes of lightning. The chilly wind whipped the electric wires around the courtyard. Shivering in my raincoat, I tried hard to keep my eyes open in the cold rain.

Comrade Li cleared his throat and the whispering stopped instantly.

"I've been informed that Niu and a group of traitors tried to defect to Hong Kong. Alert soldiers from our People's Liberation Army captured all, except Niu." He paused and glared at us.

My legs weakened from fear. I leaned against Father's arm.

"Anyone who escapes from our motherland is betraying our great leader, Chairman Mao. Niu is our enemy! If you have any information about him, come to me immediately. Or you, too, will be the people's enemy."

My chest felt stuffed with cotton; I could hardly breathe. If only I had told my parents, maybe they could have stopped Niu. I hated myself for keeping the secret from them.

Maybe he was in Hong Kong with his uncle now. Soon he would fly to America. I thought of the Golden Gate Bridge. I wished I could be there.

When we were back home, Mother wept. Father led her to their bedroom. I wasn't sure if I should tell them I knew about Niu's secret. I decided to wait until Mother wasn't so upset.

That night, I tossed and turned in bed like a fish in a net. I awoke to heavy pounding. I jumped out of bed and peeked from behind my bedroom door. Short Legs and Mouse Eyes stormed into our living room.

"What can I do for you?" Father asked sternly. He was in his yellow cotton pajamas.

"We caught Niu. Come with us," Mouse Eyes snarled.

Father grabbed a jacket and hurried out after them.

My heart filled with joy. Niu was alive! But relief turned to worry. Was he hurt? Would they let him come home? It must be. Otherwise, why would they get Father? It had been over two months since I last saw him.

Without changing out of my pajamas, I slipped on my overcoat and set up the folding bed near the fireplace. After covering it with the softest blanket from my bed, I ran to the kitchen to light the stove. Niu might like a hot bath after he got home.

Mother had given me a lesson on how to light our

coal stove. It was shaped like a bucket with a small door. Inside, about halfway down, it had a grate. To light it, first put a handful of wood chips in the center, then set the egg-size coal pieces on top, and quickly fan air into the open door.

When I tried, the wood chips went out without lighting the coal on top. I spread more chips around the coal. This time only smoke came out. My eyes stung and my throat felt like it was being poked by small fish bones. Just when I was running out of ideas, Father came back. Niu was not with him.

"Where is Niu?" I ran to him.

Father took out his handkerchief and wiped ashes off my face. The sadness in his eyes made him seem older.

"Tell me, Daddy." I shook his arm. "Is Niu okay? Is he coming home?"

Father swallowed. "Niu is okay. But he's not coming back."

"Why?" I cried.

Mother came in with a basketful of vegetables, a few eggs nested on top. "What happened?" she asked, wiping sweat from her forehead with a handkerchief.

"They caught Niu in the river and brought him back late last night." Father sat down heavily in a chair. "Five Red Guards interrogated him all night. Today he drew a class line and denounced his parents and us as his enemies." Father stared at the floor with tears in his eyes. "In exchange, Comrade Li will let him stay in the city and present him to the neighborhood as a model revolutionary who turned against the evil bourgeoisie."

Mother's basket struck the floor. Vegetables spilled over, and one egg broke. "What's happening to all of us?" She burst out crying.

"Why, Daddy?" I shouted. "What have we done to become his enemy?" I thought of Father's coat and my precious chocolate.

Without anwering me, Father got up and went into his bedroom.

What did "draw a class line" mean? After one of the boys in our courtyard drew a class line, he joined the Red Guards and his parents were sent away. Would Niu keep the secrets we shared? Would they have hurt him if he hadn't drawn a class line? The thought of Niu calling me his enemy made me believe I could never be happy again.

That afternoon, coming home from school, I saw a huge poster by the hospital entrance. My eyes blurred in the bright sunlight. The characters were written in red ink.

DEAR MOTHER, DEAR FATHER,
BUT NOBODY IS AS DEAR AS CHAIRMAN MAO. . . .

I sped up, squeezing past a crowd in front of it, my thoughts racing. I'd never met Chairman Mao. I doubted he would take care of me when I was sick or sing English songs with me. He could never be dearer than my parents.

Dark Clouds

After the three janitors in the hospital were praised as the working class, they no longer had to do their work. Instead, they gave political lectures at meetings and oversaw the Revolution. Now it became Father's job to clean the whole hospital.

Each night, Father came home dirty and tired. When he walked in the door, I ran to fetch his slippers and set them in front of his chair. "Are you tired, Daddy?"

"Never!" He slapped his chest and flexed his arm muscles. "I am a tireless horse."

I asked him one time, "Do you hate cleaning bathrooms and mopping floors?"

Father smiled. "It's good exercise. I played soccer in college and always slept soundly after a good workout."

But Father's work didn't seem to help him sleep. In the middle of the night, when I awoke from bad dreams, I'd find him sitting in his chair tying knots with Mother's sewing thread. He was keeping up his surgical skills. Father had shown me how to tie surgeon's knots. Occasionally, he stopped and gazed out the dark window as if searching for something. Once I heard him softly reciting the words of the calligraphy.

> *A great physician should not pay attention to status, wealth, or age. Nor should he question whether his patient is an enemy or friend. . . .*

One day in late October, Father didn't come home until long past dinnertime. Mother sent me to look for him at the hospital.

The long corridor leading to the emergency room reeked of mildew and urine. As I passed the toilet, I held my breath.

The hallway was lit by one bare bulb. An old man sat on a long bench, hiccuping like a sick rooster unable to swallow. A young woman held up a hand wrapped with a piece of blood-soaked cloth.

I ran past them and turned in to the brightly lit emergency room. I was surprised to see Father sewing up a cut on a boy's head, while a young doctor stood next to him.

"Give him one antibiotic shot and change the bandage every other day."

The young doctor nodded like an obedient student.

Father peeled off his gloves and grasped the long handle of a heavy mop. "Now back to the bathroom. It's been ignored all afternoon."

On the way home, I asked Father if he would get into more trouble if Comrade Li found out. I was worried because Comrade Li seemed to be getting more and more powerful. Every day he gave orders through the loudspeaker.

"Don't worry! He can't harm me." Father patted my shoulder.

On my eleventh birthday, Father managed to take a half day off work. He met me at school. We walked down to the riverbank and sat on the stone step. In front of us, the Han River joined the swift Yangtze. It had rained the week before, so the river was wider than usual and covered most of the white beach.

Across the riverbank, a candy factory's two-story building looked like a toy house spitting out dark smoke. The air smelled of sweet ginger. The sun peeked through the gray clouds now and then. Boats passing by on the river blew their horns.

At that moment, I no longer cared about my worries. Even though I wouldn't get any new clothes for my birthday, I felt happy just sitting next to Father.

"Ling, can you recite the Samuel Coleridge poem?"

"Of course, Daddy."

"Are you sure?" Father widened his smiling eyes.

I knew Father had heard me practice the poem all week.

I turned and faced him. His gray jacket had a rectangular patch on the right shoulder. Below was a small button with Chairman Mao's portrait. Behind him, on the riverbank, a team of men unloaded timber from a blue boat. The wind occasionally blew their revolutionary work song to us. I cleared my throat and began.

> *Do you ask what the birds say? The Sparrow,*
> *the Dove,*
> *The Linnet and Thrush say "I love, and I love!"*

In the winter they're silent—the wind is so strong,
What it says, I don't know, but it sings a loud
   song.
But green leaves, and blossoms, and sunny warm
   weather . . .

I stopped. I couldn't believe what I saw.

"What's next, Ling? That was wonderful!"

"Daddy, look!" I pointed behind him.

A man was walking into the river with his clothes on. The water was up to his chest.

Father ran, and I ran after him. A wave came. The man disappeared into the muddy water. Without hesitation, Father jumped into the river fully clothed.

I yelled at the blue boat, "Help, help! Someone is drowning."

The workers stopped what they were doing.

"Give me a life ring," I screamed.

One man wearing only a pair of red shorts threw down a ring. I snatched it and stumbled along the shore.

For a moment I could see someone's head above the water, but he soon disappeared again.

"Daddy!" I ran into the water. "Catch it, Daddy!" I

threw the ring as hard as I could. The water pushed it swiftly past Father. I wished Mother had let me learn to swim like Niu!

Someone grabbed my sleeve. "You want to die?" It was the man with red shorts. "The water is too strong. It'll sweep you away."

With his tight grip, he dragged me back to the riverbank. I turned to the workers standing behind me and screamed as loudly as I could, "Help them! Help my father!"

Two of the workers waded into the river. Father rose to the surface, his arm supporting the man's head. The workers grabbed the man around his waist and dragged him toward the bank.

After staggering ashore, Father fell to his hands and knees.

I ran to him. The workers laid the drowning man on his back. The man's eyes were closed and his stomach bulged.

"He is dead," one bald worker commented in a panicked voice. "He's not breathing."

Father struggled to reach the man. I put my hands under Father's arm to support him. He flipped the man onto his stomach and pounded on his back. Yellow water poured out of his mouth, then he choked and coughed. Feeling goose bumps on my forearms, I swallowed the urge to throw up.

Father pulled the man to a sitting position. A moment later, his eyes blinked half open, reminding me of the eyes of a dead fish.

In a shrieking voice, the worker in red shorts pointed at the soggy man and yelled, "I saw his picture in the newspaper. Isn't he the antirevolutionary writer?"

"Yes. I saw his picture, too. I remember his eyes," said a worker in a white T-shirt. "He wrote antirevolutionary articles. Let him die!"

I stood there shocked, watching them walk away. Within a few minutes, only Father and I were there with the nearly drowned writer.

How could they just leave him to die? Father almost lost his life to save him. Would they come back to arrest the man? Suddenly, the man spoke, in the perfect Mandarin of someone from Beijing. "Please! I'd rather die my way than let them kill me."

"Don't talk like that. You need food and dry clothes."

Father placed the writer's arm over his shoulder and helped him to stand. He was tall. A white shirt clung to his chest, and his blue pants were barely held on by a leather belt. I noticed that on his long face, one of his eyes was larger than the other.

"No, no. Leave me alone. I'll only bring you trouble."

"Don't worry. We live nearby." Father motioned me to help.

I lifted the writer's other wet, sticklike arm over my shoulder.

It had never seemed to take so long to walk home from the river. As we crossed the wide Six-Port Revolutionary Road, we had to wait for a tractor loaded with live chickens to pass. A group of people in blue uniforms followed on bicycles. VICTORY SHIPPING GROUP was printed on their jackets. They slowed down their pedaling and cranked the bells on their handlebars at us. For a frightening moment, I feared they would get off their bicycles and pull the writer away. His wet arm now felt as heavy as an iron bar on my shoulder.

Once we turned into Red Horse Alley, leading to the back door of our courtyard, the air reeked of gasoline and fried garlic. Families squatted beside front doors while eating dinner. When we passed, they stopped chewing and stared.

As soon as we were in our apartment, the man

spoke again. "I am Ji, the antirevolutionary writer they spoke of—"

Father put his hand on the writer's shoulder. "It's not important. Rest. I will get you some food and dry clothes."

Since everything was rationed, we didn't have much to offer. I ran to our kitchen, climbed on a chair in front of the pantry, and found all the shelves empty. Standing on tiptoes, I peered deeper inside. There! A small package.

Carefully, I removed the oiled paper wrapping.

Father asked, "What's that?"

It took a moment before I could speak. "It's d-dried shrimp." I tried hard not to cry. "Mrs. Wong gave them to us."

Father hugged me. "It's okay, my dear. Everything will be fine."

I closed my eyes and wished that when I opened them again I'd be sitting at our dinner table enjoying a feast with Mother, Father, beautiful Mrs. Wong, serious Dr. Wong, and brother Niu.

Father put a spoonful of loose tea into a mug and filled it with hot water from a dented red thermos. I held the mug with two hands and brought it to Mr. Ji.

The sun broke through the clouds, leaving a long shiny patch on the living room floor. Sitting at the dinner table, he now wore Father's clothes. Two middle buttons on the shirt were undone. When I put the tea in front of him, his dull eyes continued staring at the strip of writing on the wall—BOURGEOIS SYMPATHIZERS.

I ran back to the kitchen. Father was about to empty a bag of dried noodles into a pot of boiling water.

"Wait, Daddy." I opened our rice jar and dug down. "Remember, Mommy always says old ginger helps to prevent a cold?" I fished out a wrinkly piece. "Put some in his noodles."

"Smart girl," Father said in English. He chopped up the hardened ginger. I dropped the pieces into the water and then poured in the noodles. At last, I sprinkled in a handful of dried shrimp. Father smiled at me. Only then did I notice he was still in his wet clothes.

"Daddy, you'll catch cold. Go change."

"No hurry, Ling. Let's first serve our guest." He poured the noodles into a big bowl and carried it to Mr. Ji. I followed with a pair of bamboo chopsticks and a spoon.

"Sorry we don't have anything better to serve you," said Father.

"I am leaving now. It's dangerous to have me in your home."

"Please eat." Father set the bowl before him on the table.

I put the chopsticks and spoon next to it.

Mr. Ji's eyes shifted between Father and the bowl of steaming noodles. He touched the chopsticks but didn't lift them.

I wondered if he was hungry. Had he eaten a big meal before walking into the river?

"Please eat while it's still hot," urged Father.

Tugging gently on my sleeve, Father led me to the kitchen. He whispered, "I'm going to change. Give Mr. Ji a moment to himself."

I waited until Father returned to the kitchen in dry clothes. Together, we went to the living room.

Mr. Ji stood up immediately, the bowl in front of him now empty. He grasped Father's hands and said slowly, "They can kill me, but not the truth."

Father nodded and said, "Promise me you'll live."

"I will try. But dark clouds have concealed the sun

for too long." Mr. Ji didn't let go of Father's hand until they reached the door.

I ran to the window and watched him walk into the sun.

Shortly after Mr. Ji left, Mother rushed into the house as if running from a flood. She whispered between heavy breaths, "The whole hospital is talking about you two saving an antirevolutionary writer."

"Did we?" Father winked at me.

With my mouth and eyes opened wide, I smiled at him. "We did!"

"*Ai yo!*" said Mother. "You are two melons on the same vine."

I felt proud to be from the same vine as Father. *I love you, brave Daddy!* I whispered to myself.

Would I Ever See Him Again?

The winter months seemed endless. Cold and hungry, days and nights mixed together. Father didn't get his wish to return to surgery. To keep warm, he dressed in layers of old jackets under his long blue hospital coat.

What would it take to end this misery? When we looked at the picture of the Golden Gate Bridge by candlelight, Father whispered, "Never give up hope, my dear. Life can't go on like this forever. Someday we will be free of this injustice." Father hid the picture behind Chairman Mao's portrait again.

But it felt like it had already gone on forever.

To celebrate Christmas Eve, Mother made dumplings stuffed with onions and soybeans. Although I missed her juicy pork-cabbage filling, I was happy to have enough to eat. I felt cheerful in our brightly lit apartment. It had been weeks since we last had electricity. The windows around the apartment were covered with a layer of white mist from cooking.

After helping Mother take the dirty dishes to the kitchen, I tiptoed to the door that separated our home from Comrade Li's. Flattening my face against the crack at the hinge, I saw that it was dark inside.

Father sat in his chair, where the slashed leather was now patched up with white bandages. His eyes followed me. I shook my head. With one finger, he tapped his ear. I pressed my ear to the door.

A week before, Comrade Li's room had been dark. Father and I thought he was not there. As we got ready for our English lesson, Mother came home and told us that she had seen Comrade Li walk out of his dark apartment toward the bathroom.

I made sure I heard no breathing or the floor creaking on the other side before I shook my head again.

As part of this week's English lesson, I was learning to sing "Red River Valley."

Outside, soundless lightning streaked the sky. In the distance, a boat passed and blew its horn.

Father nodded. I walked toward him and sang quietly.

> *As you go to your home by the ocean,*
> *May you never forget those sweet hours*

I wrapped my arms around his shoulders. Father tapped his fingers on the armrest and joined in with his deep voice.

> *That we spent in the Red River Valley.*

A dog in the neighborhood began barking. All of a sudden, footsteps drummed on the stairs. Father stood. Mother ran in from the kitchen.

Our door was kicked open. Six Red Guards stormed in holding fighting sticks. I held Father's hand tightly and couldn't help trembling.

It took a minute for me to believe my eyes! Niu was among them. He wore a Red Guard uniform and held a wide belt with a shiny buckle. His glasses were gone—perhaps to look less bourgeois. Squinting his eyes into small lines, he roamed around like a hungry dog sniffing out a bone.

"Search every corner." He swung his belt around in the middle of our living room. The Red Guards ran in all directions. The noise of sticks smashing furniture, breaking dishes, and tearing clothes came from all directions. "You"—he pointed at Father without looking at him—"are under arrest for sympathizing with the antirevolutionary writer." Spit flew about as he spoke, and he sounded nervous. He didn't address Father as Uncle like he always did. His face was bloodless, and tiny beads of sweat oozed on his stubby nose.

Father's eyes met Niu's, but Niu quickly turned away. It reminded me of the time when Father caught him using his scalpels to cut out paper turtles. Father let go of my hand, took off his watch, and stuffed it into Mother's pocket. "Trade it for food," he said in his low, firm voice.

Mother broke out crying.

"Please, Niu," she begged. "We love you! Don't take your uncle away." Father stopped her with his eyes.

Niu glanced toward the half-opened front door

and smashed his belt down onto the dinner table. The large metal buckle left a deep scar. His shaking hand pointed to the portrait over the fireplace, and he shouted, "The only one who loves me is Chairman Mao!" He sounded like a kicked dog. His finger slid up the bridge of his nose to push up eyeglasses that weren't there.

Cold sweat soaked the back of my blouse. I bit my lip to keep myself from crying. The thought of them taking Father and making him disappear like Dr. Wong horrified me. If they took me with Father, at least I would know where he was.

I stepped in front of Niu. "Take me, too. I was part of it." I searched for friendship in his eyes, but I saw only anger.

Father pulled me back by my arm. He whispered in my ear, "Take care of Mommy. Remember, GGB."

Niu stepped between us and handcuffed Father.

Short Legs reported to Niu, "Comrade Wong, we can't find any antirevolutionary materials."

"I will show you." Niu turned and went to the radio. I gasped as he ripped out a handful of wires and tubes. He dropped them on the floor and crushed them under his boot. I knew this time that the radio could never be repaired.

Niu looked around our living room and took a step toward the portrait of Chairman Mao, which hid the Golden Gate Bridge.

Was he going to destroy the picture? I ran behind him and grabbed his belt forcefully. "Take me with my father! I am an antirevolutionary, too."

Niu turned and pushed me. "Get away from me."

I tripped and fell to the floor. Father came to help me, but his hands were cuffed. I quickly stood up and forced back my tears. I didn't want Father to worry, and I didn't want to appear weak.

Pimple Face pushed Father aside. I saw pain in Father's eyes.

Mother broke into short, rapid sobs.

"Time to go," Niu ordered.

Father gazed around the softly lit room as if to store each object in his memory. As he was pushed out the door by Pimple Face and Short Legs, he called out, "Be strong. Take care of each other."

I ran after them. Mother grabbed me at the doorway. There stood Comrade Li in the dim hallway, his smile lit up by his glowing cigarette. I slammed the door in his face. Mother went into her bedroom and closed the door behind her.

I walked across the messy apartment, sat in Father's chair, and hugged myself. Not until now did I let tears run down my cheeks, salty streams rolling onto my lips. Angry with myself, I wished I had thought of a way to make them arrest me along with Father.

The days seemed so much longer without Father. In the morning, I could barely get up, knowing he wasn't there. I missed his cheerful voice waking me. At night, I kept one of his old scarves next to my pillow, hoping his smell would bring him into my dreams. But the only dream I had was of people waving scissors at me. I longed for Father's comforting words when I awoke from nightmares, fearing that the Red Guards would cut my hair like they did Mrs. Wong's. Worst of all, there was no one I could talk to.

Mother stopped criticizing me, as if she didn't care what I did anymore. Working nights in the emergency room, she spent most days hidden in the apartment. She walked like a frightened cat, making no sounds, freezing in the middle of her movements. Before letting me leave for school, she hid behind the kitchen curtain, rubbing the third button on her jacket continuously, and inspected the courtyard as if she expected someone waiting there to take me away.

I knew better than to tell her that a week ago Gao and Yu attacked me in the middle of narrow Flower Alley. They broke my pencils and tore up my Chinese dictionary. They would have torn up all my books, too, if a woman hadn't thrown dirty water at them from her doorway. She yelled, "Noisy brats! Take your fight elsewhere."

The hospital had stopped paying Father's salary. Without his income, Mother and I had to make everything last longer, especially things that were rationed: food, soap, toothpaste, sugar, cooking oil, even toilet paper. We could no longer afford to buy candles on the black market.

After Mother went to work at night, I stayed near my bedroom window, writing and drawing by streetlight. On scrap paper Mother brought home from the hospital, I wrote down things I wanted to tell Father. I used the English words and phrases I knew. It made me feel as if he was right there with me.

I had read in my history book that before Chairman Mao took over China, his underground Communists wrote secret notes with rice water and would later brush iodine on the paper to make the words reappear. I decided to try it. I filled one of my fountain pens with rice water and wrote and drew on whatever I could find: torn wallpaper, Mao's instruction sheets, and the backs of envelopes. Once dried, the words were invisible. I planned to make them reappear when Father came home. All my poems were sad.

> *Through the frosty window,*
> *I look upon the moon and ask*
> *Can my dear Father see you at this moment?*
> *Please send him home.*

Soon I had a pillowcase filled with invisible writing and drawings. I was glad I no longer had to destroy them.

On Chinese New Year's Eve, Mother set out a bowl of rice covered with vegetables and two golden pan-fried eggs. My stomach rumbled. It had been months since I had had an egg. I ran to get two pairs of chopsticks. But Mother had her own plans.

"This is all for you," she said as she lit the almost empty oil lamp. "I must go to work. I will eat there. Blow out the light before you go to bed." She rubbed the button on her jacket as she walked toward the door.

"But, Mother. . . ." I wanted to say, *Please have dinner with me. I am afraid and lonely in the dark after you go to work.* My pride stopped me from begging her. The hospital's dining hall closed over the New Year holiday. Where would she find food to eat?

"I'm late. Go to bed early." Mother locked the door behind her.

I waited until I heard her footsteps on the stairs, then ran to the kitchen window and watched her drag herself down. Outside, children cheered as fireworks went off. Next door, Comrade Li was hosting a dinner party. They shouted Chairman Mao's quotations and sang revolutionary songs. The smell of fried dumplings wafted into our empty apartment. Our oil lamp gave out a faint orange light. The living room was as dark as a movie theater. I stared at Mao's portrait above the fireplace. Mice scuttled above the ceiling, making scratching sounds. I envied the baby mice. They must have felt safe and happy to be with their parents. Tears rolled down my face.

Last year, on Chinese New Year's Eve, one of Father's patients brought us fresh lotus roots from his commune. Mother made lotus soup with pig bones. She set our small coal stove in the middle of the living room and simmered the soup all day. The flavorful smell filled the apartment and turned all the windows foggy. During dinner, Father showed me how to stick my chopsticks inside the hollow bones to dig out the marrow. It was delicious! That meal kept me warm the rest of the evening.

Now we no longer had money to buy extra coal to heat the apartment. The furniture was icy to the touch. The heavy cotton jacket weighted me down, and the biting cold left my hands and feet numb.

Seeing the eggs in my bowl cheered me up. Mother had even flavored them with soy sauce. Since food had been rationed, she rarely used the expensive seasoning. I longed to taste the crisp egg whites and sink my teeth into the creamy yolk. Not wanting to waste even the smell, I sniffed at them until my mouth watered. I took a bite and chewed extra long, keeping it in my mouth until the flavor was gone. They were the most delicious eggs I ever tasted.

Outside the courtyard, a siren screamed. I stopped chewing, hoping they were not taking away someone else's father. The fire in the lamp jumped a few times, then went out. I moved next to the window in my bedroom and decided to draw the girl in the sun hat on the blouse that Mrs. Wong had made for me. I kept it hidden between layers of my bed's cotton batting.

The streetlight threw tree branch shadows on my bed, as if spreading long ghost fingers. Peeling the top two layers back, I was shocked to find the blouse was gone. I searched my room and the whole apartment again and again, wishing magic would happen and my blouse would reappear.

I thrust my arm deep between the layers under the cotton batting in Mother's bed. I cried out with joy when my fingertips touched something. What I pulled out was white hospital bandages wound together into a long rope.

I puzzled over what this was. A clothesline to replace the split bamboo rod? Or perhaps it was for tying up the winter blankets for storage over the summer. I put the rope back and wondered again about my blouse.

Nobody had come to our home since Father was taken away. Where could my blouse be? A week ago, I had taken it out and admired it. Though it was too small for me now, it brought back so many happy memories.

A terrible thought came to my mind. Mother had been taking our belongings to the black market to trade for coal and rice. Had she traded it for things? Maybe people from the countryside could still wear clothes with bright colors.

That night seemed to never end. Mother wouldn't trade my blouse without asking me, would she? When the sky outside the window turned pale, Mother came home with a slightly swollen face.

Running up to her, I tried to sound as sweet as I could. "Momma, do you know where my blouse is? I hid it under my mattress."

As she walked toward her bedroom, she said with a blank expression, "I traded it for the eggs you ate yesterday."

"How could you do that?" I cried.

Mother closed the bedroom door behind her.

My sobs echoed in the apartment. How could she trade my blouse without asking? I stomped, hoping the noise would bring her back out. But the door stayed closed.

I ran to my room and pressed Father's scarf to my face, hoping the last bit of his smell would give me comfort.

The Long White Rope

The days slowly moved on. Mother and I struggled to get enough to eat, coal for our little stove, oil for the lamp, and water for cooking and washing. Yet we rarely spoke to each other.

Outside, green buds quietly turned to full leaves on the milk trees. One morning after work, instead of going to her room, Mother sat down at the table. "Come here, Ling. I need to talk to you."

I was so pleased that she wanted to talk. There were so many things I wanted to say to her. I wanted to tell her she was the only person I had left in the world. And I wanted her to know I even forgave her for trading my precious blouse.

"Listen carefully." Mother placed a list on the table. "You're almost twelve now, and you need to learn how to do these chores." Her bloodshot eyes stared at me like a pair of daggers. I looked away.

She paused for a moment, rubbing the button on her jacket, as if deciding how to tell me the rest. "In case I am gone—"

"What do you mean, in case you are gone? I'm too young to be by myself."

Mother's glazed eyes stared at Chairman Mao's portrait above the fireplace.

"Answer me, Mother . . . please!" I started to cry.

She continued. "Soak the dirty clothes first before putting on the soap. Use the washboard—"

"I don't want to hear it. I'm too young to learn." I ran to my room and closed the door.

I shivered with fear. My mouth let out all the bad words I knew. Outside my window, three sparrows drummed their wings. I wished I could fly away from this miserable place. What did Mother mean by "in case I am gone"? Were they going to take her away, too? Or was she going to try to kill herself by walking into the river like Mr. Ji?

The sparrows shot away. Someone staggered into the courtyard. I recognized her as the doctor known for delivering babies. On one side of her head, the hair had been cut close to the scalp and the other half was shoulder-length. A streak of blood flowed from her forehead. One of the sleeves was missing from her white sweater, showing her bare arm. She was approaching the three-story building across the courtyard when Mother joined me at the window.

"Oh, no! They gave her a yin-yang haircut at today's public criticism meeting," Mother whispered. Her fingers reached again for her button.

Fear and pain stirred in my chest. What crime could the baby doctor have committed? I'd always seen her either holding a baby or walking with a pregnant woman. Were they afraid she would turn babies into antirevolutionaries? An awful thought filled me. Would Mother be strong enough to endure a public criticism meeting? Did she tell me "in case I am gone" because she believed something was going to happen to her?

Soon, the doctor's two teenage sons and their grandmother rushed into the courtyard from the street. The skinny grandmother stumbled on her tiny crippled feet. Mother had told me that in the old days girls were forced to bind their feet to keep them small.

The older boy had a little black mole on the left side of his chin and was half a head taller than the younger one, who had a wide face and flat nose. They both were strongly built. The family had moved in about a year ago. I had overheard that their father had died of cancer.

Now the boys were on each side of their grandmother, helping her along. Their faces were pinched with worry. A moment after they went in their building, I heard the grandmother's wailing. The older boy ran out screaming, "Help! Help my mother!"

Mother clutched my arms with both her hands. Just when I was trying to decide if I should break away from her grip to help the doctor, Comrade Li ran into the courtyard, followed by Pink Cheeks, Short Legs, Pimple Face, and Mouse Eyes. His amplified voice shrieked through the loudspeaker at the boy. "Get your antirevolutionary mother down here now!" The boy froze for a second, then ran back inside the building. Short Legs, Pimple Face, and Pink Cheeks chased after him.

Mother let go of me and ran into her room. I hurried after her and found her shivering on the floor, leaning against her bed, eyes closed. "They are coming for me! They are coming for me! It's my turn now!" she murmured.

Hiding my fear, I cupped her face in my hands and said gently, "Mom, Mom, they are coming for the baby doctor, not you! Not you!" She slowly opened her eyes and looked at me without blinking.

"Everyone report to the courtyard at once! To the courtyard now!" Comrade Li's angry voice cut through our closed windows. Mother let me move her about like a puppet. I helped her put on her jacket and go down to the courtyard.

To our horror, there in front of the doctor's building lay a stretcher covered with a blue sheet, a body outlined beneath it.

What was underneath the sheet? The baby doctor's body? How could that be? She had just run across the courtyard. I didn't want to believe what I saw.

The two sons supported the unsteady grand-mother, standing next to the stretcher. She wept vigorously, and tears trickled down her cheeks. She seemed about to fall to the ground if not for the two boys. The older boy kept wiping his puffy eyes with the back of his free hand. The younger one stared into the distance, as if his mind was far away.

My heart trembled with fear and sadness. If they took her to the hospital now, could she be saved? I pushed my tears back. I didn't want Comrade Li to see them.

Surrounded by Red Guards, Comrade Li stood next to the older boy, smoking his cigarette as he waited for everyone to assemble. When he noticed us, he gave me an evil leering grin. Mother kept her eyes half closed.

About twenty neighbors stood silent in the cold spring wind. It had rained the day before, so the ground of the courtyard was muddy. Small puddles had formed in a few places. Branches stretched to the sky like desperate arms, pleading for help.

Comrade Li shouted through the loudspeaker. "Everyone, take a close look at the number one traitor!" He pointed at the figure beneath the sheet. "By committing suicide," he continued, "she refused to be reeducated and showed her hatred for Chairman Mao and the Revolution!"

Why did the doctor kill herself? Did she do it because they cut her hair and tore her clothes? Could I have done something to save her? My vision blurred.

"Show your love for Chairman Mao. Draw a class line between yourselves and this traitor," Comrade Li shrieked at the doctor's family.

"Never!" The older boy thrust up his fist and spat at Comrade Li's face. "You drove her to this. You killed my mother!" The black mole on his chin moved up and down as he cried. Surprised, Comrade Li backed up a few steps and wiped the spit off with his sleeve. The whole courtyard fell silent. I could hear Mother's heavy breathing. From the river, a boat sounded its horn and gave out several short blasts. My head pounded.

"You antirevolutionary insect!" Comrade Li lifted his metal loudspeaker and smashed it down on the boy's head. It gave out the clanking sound of metal hitting rock, followed by a short squeal of static. Blood gushed from a cut above the boy's ear. He fell to his knees, dragging down his grandmother, who struggled to remain standing and then collapsed on the ground beside him.

It felt like someone was kicking me from the inside.

"I'll teach him a lesson." Pimple Face furiously kicked the boy as he fell flat on the ground, groaning. Mouse Eyes stomped on his chest. Blood flowed from his mouth. His arms and legs stretched in and out as if pulled by invisible ghosts.

Tears welled in my eyes. Shivering, I gasped for breath. A young nurse standing next to me began sobbing. Mother wrapped her arm around my shoulder. I could feel her weight on me. I wished someone would stop the beating. If Father was here, he'd save the boy like he saved Mrs. Wong.

Suddenly, the grandmother threw herself over the boy. She pleaded in her high-pitched voice, "Please, please forgive us. We will draw a class line between us and my antirevolutionary daughter. Forgive my grandson. I will take my daughter's place to be re-educated."

The beating stopped. The air smelled of blood. A

few drops of cold rain fell on my face. How could they cruelly beat the boy after he had just lost his mother? The grandmother must have felt so desperate to denounce her daughter to save her grandsons.

Looking around me, many women had their eyes shut like Mother. Three young doctors stood in a far corner, their faces tightened with anger. I wished they would do something to stop this! But no one moved. They must be afraid to bring trouble to themselves and their family.

Pimple Face wedged his club between the grandmother and the wounded boy. He stabbed her chest with his stick until she fell backward. Now the older boy lay there motionless, covered with dust. The younger boy lifted his grandmother to her knees. Tears trickled down his face.

The hair on my arms bristled, and I tried hard to push down the lump in my throat.

As the Red Guards dragged the two boys away, the grandmother threw herself on top of the body on the stretcher and wailed, "Why did you have to do this? Didn't you know your boys would have to pay for your death?"

It was then I realized that death could not end the suffering. Would the baby doctor still have killed herself if she had known what would happen to her family?

As Short Legs and Mouse Eyes dragged the grandmother away, she gripped the blue sheet, and it trailed along behind her, revealing the baby doctor's body. An old man broke into long howls of despair, sounding like an injured wolf. It echoed around the courtyard. The ground underneath me swayed. I gripped the milk tree for support.

A long white rope, just like the one under Mother's mattress, was tied around the baby doctor's neck. Her eyes were wide open.

Shopping with Mother

All summer, the baby doctor's vacant face haunted me. In my dreams, she walked toward me with a white rope around her neck, carrying a baby in her arms. As I stretched my hand to take the baby, she faded away. I often woke in a cold sweat and couldn't fall back to sleep. I lingered over the fear of what Mother planned to do with the rope under her bed. I wanted to take it away from her, but when I went to look for it, it was gone.

I couldn't stop thinking about the two boys and the grandmother. I never saw them again after that horrible day.

Was the older boy able to recover from the beating? I had seen him around the hospital compound many times before. Except for the mole on his face,

I thought he was handsome, especially his double-lidded eyes. When we had passed by each other in the courtyard, he'd look down, avoiding eye contact with me. I had sensed a sadness in him, which made me curious. Was he sad because he lost his father? Did he love his father as much as I loved mine? I wished I'd had the courage to talk to him and get to know him. Deep down, I hoped I could be as brave as he was when the time came to defend Mother.

I learned to do many chores. Mother hadn't talked about going away again, but the thought of her rope still cast a shadow over me. I feared any misbehavior would make her leave me. I had grown tall and skinny. Would Father recognize me if he saw me in my patched-up Mao jacket?

When the fall rain turned to sleet, crusting the ground with ice, I learned from the newspaper that workers at the water plant worked only half days, using the rest of the time to study Mao's teachings. When they were at work, they didn't do a good job. The faucet in our kitchen dripped sandy water only at night. I wrapped two layers of surgical pads over the spout and in a day or two they filled with sand.

We kept our enamel washbasin under the faucet to catch drops at night. By morning, it was often only half full and covered with a thin skin of ice. I broke the ice with a metal spatula. On the bottom of the basin was a drawing of the sun surrounded by lines of words in red paint: LONG LIVE CHAIRMAN MAO! LONG LIVE CHAIRMAN MAO! One "Long" had faded off. I doubted Mao had to wash his face with cold, sandy water.

I learned to save water by first washing my face, then clothes, and last, mopping the floor.

I had become skilled at using a washboard—a wooden board carved with deep grooves. I pressed and rolled the clothes up and down on it. My hands grew numb in the icy water, and the small pieces of soap slipped out of my swollen fingers.

Many times, I promised myself that when I grew up, if bars of soap were no longer rationed, I would buy a box of them and use only the large pieces. If Mother still thought someone should use the small pieces, I'd save them for her. Then she would know how hard it was.

One chore Mother hadn't asked me to do was shop in the market. She said I was still too young to fight for food. I couldn't imagine how bad it might be. The days when she came home with an empty basket, I wished she had taken me with her. I would have bought anything edible to stop the hunger.

Finally, one Sunday in early February, she woke me.

"Hurry! There is meat today. I'll show you how to shop."

I opened my eyes. It was still dark outside.

"Now? What time is it?"

"Three-thirty in the morning," Mother answered in her tired voice. I reached for my coat on top of my cotton blankets. The chill forced me to pull my hand back under the warm blankets. But the thought of Mother deciding I was old enough to shop in the market drove me to sit up. I took a deep breath and slipped into my ice-cold jacket.

Outside, thick fog swallowed us. The air felt damp. The streetlights gave out a soft yellow glow. Torn posters snapped in the chilly breeze. I couldn't help shivering. My ears ached. Under layers of clothes, I couldn't reach my itchy back. It had been weeks since my last bath. I dreamed of soaking in hot water and scrubbing off the grimy smell from my body. To keep my frostbitten hands warm, I tried to tuck them into opposite sleeves, but only the tips of my swollen fingers fit in.

The market was on the way to school. I'd never been there so early. Mother often shopped after her night shift. During the day, the shelves were empty. Occasionally, a line of cardboard boxes sat on the sales counters with notes on top. Once, when no one was in the shop, I went in to look. Names were written on the notes. Inside were clean vegetables, eggs, and chunks of meat. One of them was addressed to Comrade Li.

The fat saleslady had rushed from behind and yelled at me, "Get away! No more food today."

I shot her a disgusted look and ran. What did she mean, no food? Were those boxes only for powerful people?

I had never seen so many people near the shop as there were this morning. A long, twisted line started two blocks away. No wonder Mother rarely brought meat home.

"Any meat today?" Mother asked the last person in line. He was wrapped up in a gray scarf, only showing his eyes.

"Who knows? I saw them unload a rickshaw of meat half an hour ago. But this snake line hasn't moved." He stamped his feet to keep warm. "I suppose it depends on whether or not they have enough for the back door." His voice cracked with anger. People sat on the concrete street, asleep under big coats. One old man snored and wheezed like a bicycle pump. Empty baskets and big rocks sat in the line between them.

"What are those for, Mom?" I whispered and pointed to a big rock.

"People came last night and used the rocks and baskets to hold places for themselves. Everyone will come back by seven, when the shop opens," Mother explained.

I could sense angry glares following us as we moved toward the front of the line. My body tensed.

"Ah. Here's our basket." Mother pointed to a familiar bamboo basket beside a woman. "Say hello to Aunt Wu."

"Good morning, Aunt Wu."

Aunt Wu was a middle-aged woman. Her faded Mao jacket was so tight around her waist it seemed about to burst. Her buckteeth forced her upper lip to pull a little toward the right side of her face. She didn't look at me when I greeted her. Her eyes were fixed on the entrance to the shop.

Mother picked up the basket and took her place in line. "Next month it's our turn to wait in line." She said it loudly, as if she wanted to make sure Aunt Wu heard.

I had never seen Aunt Wu around the hospital. Mother must have met her at the market. As time dragged on, I stamped my feet and blew into my hands to keep them warm. My coat became damp and heavier. How had Aunt Wu stayed out in this cold all night without becoming a block of ice?

Gradually, the whole line grew restless. An old man made horrible grunting noises as he rinsed his mouth with his tea and then spat on the sidewalk. Two young women braided each other's hair.

"It starts!" yelled Aunt Wu, jutting her neck toward the entrance.

The line broke apart. People rushed toward the door. Mother held the basket in front of her, ducked her head, and pushed forward.

Someone stepped on my left shoe. Struggling to free my foot, I lost my shoe. "My shoe, my shoe!" No one paid attention to me.

Worrying I would lose the other one, I slipped it off and stuffed it into my pocket. Aunt Wu had fallen to the ground next to me.

"Give me your ration ticket and money. Let me help you." I pulled her to her feet and grabbed her basket and the roll of damp money and tickets from her hand. I pushed myself through the wall of bodies in front of me. More people pushed from behind. The force lifted me off the ground. I saw Mother ahead of me but still far from the meat counter.

When the crowd brought me back onto the ground, I slipped away to the side and ran toward the back door of the building. Something cold stuck to my socks, but I didn't stop. Soon my socks were soaked and I could no longer feel my toes.

It was much quieter at the back door, and the line was short. Only a man in an army uniform and two women stood in front of a long table set outside the shop. Small cardboard boxes sat in a row on the table. I joined the end of the line. A tall salesman in a long brown plastic apron was reading out his list. His yellow rubber gloves were soiled with blood.

"Comrade Sin, two jin."

"Coming!" I recognized the person who answered, a large uniformed man with thick caterpillar eyebrows. He was Gao's father, who had come to our school last week to announce Chairman Mao's new instructions.

Cut down on consuming and be hungry heroes
for the sake of the Cultural Revolution.

Comrade Sin took a step forward and handed one bill to the man.

The salesman handed him a small cardboard box.

"Thank you!" Whistling loudly, he walked past me. Meat and eggs peeked at me from his box.

No wonder Gao grew plump while the rest of us turned into matchsticks. At the back door, his father didn't even have to use his ration tickets. I wouldn't mind being a hungry hero either if I could eat meat and eggs. A few more customers arrived and stood in line behind me.

"Comrade Fong, one jin."

"Here!" mumbled a woman through a mouthful of bread. Her head was wrapped in a thick red scarf. As I watched her handing the salesman one bill, I admired her black nylon gloves. I longed to have a pair of warm gloves like that.

"Comrade Mong, one jin."

No one answered.

"Comrade Mong!" He studied the short line.

My head spun. From the front of the store, I heard someone scream, "No more meat! No more today!"

Had Mother ever reached the meat counter? I fumbled as I slipped the small ration ticket from the elastic band and hid it in my pocket.

"Comrade Mong—"

"Here!" I handed the salesman my paper money, focusing on his stained apron.

"Are you Comrade Mong's daughter?" The salesman stared at me.

I held my breath and nodded. My face burned with shame. If Father could see how Mother hopelessly fought in the crowd, would he forgive me for lying?

The salesman wrapped a piece of meat in a dried lotus leaf and dropped it into my basket. The meat felt as heavy as a rock. I tried to move my feet, but they didn't feel like they belonged to me. I told myself, *You can't fall. If he notices you're not wearing shoes, he'll be suspicious and take away the meat.*

Slowly, I turned and took a couple of steps.

"Come back, come back!" the salesman called from behind.

Should I run? Before I could decide what to do, I felt a gentle tap on my shoulder.

"Your change." The salesman handed me a bill. "Wake up, little girl. Next time send your father."

The crowd broke into laughter. Squeezing out a smile, I put the money in my pocket.

Would they still laugh if they knew I was the daughter of their class enemy?

When I returned to the front of the shop, people were complaining in small groups.

"I got here at eight last night," said an old man wrapped in a dirty blanket.

"Each day they take away more at the back door. We haven't had meat in two months," said a short pregnant woman.

"What's the use of having ration tickets? We still can't get any meat." A young man threw a rock to the side of the street.

"Ling, where have you been?" Mother walked toward me, her basket still empty and her sweaty hair clinging to her face. Three buttons on her now-muddy Mao jacket were missing.

The memory of Mother in her silk dress, dancing with Father, came to mind.

"Mommy, I got meat," I whispered as I held back my tears.

Aunt Wu joined us. "How did you do that?" She took the basket from me. My lost shoe was in her hand.

With a proud smile, I handed her the ration tickets and change. "You don't need tickets at the back door. And meat costs less."

Aunt Wu's face spread out like a crumpled chrysanthemum. "Smart girl!"

With tears in her eyes, Mother pulled me into her arms and hugged me tight. "You are growing up, my dear."

At that moment, I decided I would try harder to be strong and protect her, even if I had to fight or lie.

We divided the meat with Aunt Wu.

PART THREE

BRIDGE BEHIND MAO

Late Spring 1976 – Fall 1976

Angry Tiger

As time went on, I took over all the shopping duties. Mother seemed happier and less tired these days, but she forbade me from trying back-door tricks again.

"It's too dangerous, and we can't afford more trouble," she often told me.

I made no promises to her. By myself, I did whatever I could to get food for us.

When spring came, I found a safer way. I followed a group of old women from the market to a village at the edge of the city. There the villagers were selling eggs, rice, and vegetables. They were glad to sell to us, since they could charge us more than they could the government. The first time, I eagerly filled my basket with rice cakes, tofu, and carrots. But on the way home, I realized I had made a mistake. The bamboo basket grew heavier with each step. The older women were long gone, carrying their food in homemade cloth backpacks.

By the time I dragged the full basket home, my clothes and shoes were wet from the fog, and blisters covered my palms. That night, I sewed myself a backpack from Father's old jacket. I didn't show Mother my palms.

By the time my blisters turned to calluses, I had become skilled at bargaining and trading. In the village, I learned the easiest way to get the best deal was to wait until the old women bargained down the price, then haggle with the farmers for an even lower price. I usually paid less than the old women.

Using the ration tickets I'd saved, I could get soap on the black market, along with toothpaste and sometimes even brown sugar.

After one incident at the market, I learned to get hold of the goods I wanted before showing my ration tickets. A big-eared boy who was half a head taller than me offered to trade a small bag of peanuts for two of my egg ration tickets. I was so happy to see the plump peanuts. Without thinking, I took out my ration tickets hidden inside my shoe. The boy grabbed them and ran. With one shoe in hand, I chased him for two long blocks. When I caught up with him, I grabbed him by the back of his collar. I screamed and yelled and hit him with my shoe until he gave me the bag of peanuts.

That night, Mother and I enjoyed peanut and red date soup. With a smile on her face, Mother told me this soup helps the blood's circulation. I nodded and pushed down the urge to tell her how getting the peanuts had already made my blood run.

All summer I often wondered what Father would think if he saw me fighting and yelling at the market.

In the fall I began my last school year with Teacher Hui, our homeroom teacher. She had tried to protect me from Gao and his gang. Once, after Gao spat on my chair, she kept him standing in the back of the classroom all morning. When she heard Yu call me "bourgeois girl with long hair," she told Yu the length of someone's hair had nothing to do with a person being bourgeois.

Since the beginning of the semester, we had had no textbooks. Teacher Hui taught us reading from the central government's newspaper, *The People's Daily*, and the red book. In the afternoons, when she attended the teachers' political study, the Young Pioneers ran the classroom, and now Gao and Yu were in charge.

All the girls in my class had cut their hair in Jiang Qing's style, above their ears. Teacher Hui and I were the only two who still kept our hair long. I'd overheard her tell another teacher that she curled her bangs by heating an iron poker on the stove and rolling the bangs around it. I wanted to try it, but I had no bangs. Mother said I was too young for them.

This year I was finally able to make two braids the same size and weave in the loose strands. I was proud of my long hair. With everyone in the city wearing baggy Mao jackets and looking the same, I thought that with my long braids no one would mistake me for a boy.

One rainy morning, I walked into the classroom with my clothes half soaked. Gao stood behind Teacher Hui's desk. Despite all the meat and eggs his father fed him from the back door, he had only grown wider. The name Gao meant "tall," but he stood there like a big round steamed bun set on a pair of duck feet.

"Everyone, look at the poster!" Gao commanded, sniffing his runny nose. Eyeing the big piece of white paper pasted to the middle of the blackboard, he puffed up proudly and read, "Chase out the bourgeois teacher! Get educated by the working class!"

I knew better than to ask where Teacher Hui was.

Yu blocked my way with her leg as I walked to my seat. I jumped over it and ignored her. A big green gob of spit lay in the middle of my chair.

Trying hard not to show my fear and anger, I took a deep breath and reached into my bag for a piece of paper to wipe it off. Someone punched me in the back. Two paper balls hit my head. I turned. Yu, Gao, and their gang stood behind me, laughing.

I remembered Mother's words, "We can't afford more trouble." Teacher Hui was not here. No one would stop them. As I stood between my desk and the bench, they surrounded me. I had nowhere to escape.

Gao swaggered in front of my desk, waving a pair of scissors near my face. "You! Daughter of the American spy! Cut your hair, or we will do it for you!"

Punches landed on me, sending sharp pain all over. I was pushed and hit from all sides.

"Cut it now, now, now!" They cheered like cawing crows.

I swallowed to catch my breath and remained firm against the desk. Blood rushed to my head. I would rather have died than let them cut my hair.

My teeth ground in my dry mouth. "Get away from me, you stupid pigs!" The words burst out.

Gao spat. The thick spit hit my face and smelled like sour cabbage. My cheeks burned. "How dare you call us stupid pigs," Gao screamed. "I'm going to tell my father!"

"Kill the bourgeois bug now!" Yu yelled.

Within seconds, more punches landed on my shoulders and head. They pulled at my jacket so hard the buttons tore off. I tried to shield my head with one arm; the other tightly held the straps of my schoolbag. Yu grabbed my braids violently and it felt as if they were being yanked off my scalp. Gao opened and closed the scissors in the air. "Let's cut her bourgeois hair now!" His face turned dark red.

The images of Mrs. Wong's long black hair falling on the yellow leaves and the baby doctor's yin-yang haircut flashed through my thoughts.

No! I would not let them humiliate me. I would show them that I was not weak, and I would risk my life.

I swung my schoolbag fiercely against Gao's head. *Clunk! Clunk!* My abacus hit him. His eyes grew wide in surprise and pain. Once, twice! He fell over backward, knocking down the row of benches and desks behind him.

The beating stopped. The rest of them glanced at one another. I pushed my desk forcefully on top of Gao. Like an angry tiger, I roared, "I will kill you if you dare touch my hair!"

With an ear-piercing scream, Gao cried, "Help! Help! Ling is killing me! I am bleeding." His arms and legs thrashing around, he lay there tangled in desks and benches. Blood dripped from his nose. The scissors were knocked two rows away. Wiping the spit off my face with my torn sleeve, I had an urge to spit on him, but I didn't.

Yu and the others stood frozen, staring at me as if I had suddenly grown three heads. They parted, moving a few inches away from me. With my school-bag in hand, I held my head high and walked out of the classroom.

I wondered if those heroes in revolutionary movies, who'd rather die than surrender, felt as good as I did.

Too Proud to Bend

The rain had stopped, and the sun glared through wide sycamore leaves. The air was hot and humid.

I didn't want to go home. Mother would already be back from her night shift. Wandering down Big Liberation Road—the main road of the city—I thought about all the wrongs done to me.

My braids had come loose, and a few locks of long hair danced around my face in the soft breeze. The rubber bands must have been pulled off during the attack.

People dressed in dark blue and white rushed east and west on the sidewalks. A lazy snake of cars, bicycles, trucks, and rickshaws crawled slowly along the wide street. I felt the summer heat in the air. It smelled of diesel fumes and dust. I stopped in front of the Workers & Parents Department Store. A big red sign that read CLOSED FOR POLITICAL STUDIES hung on the door. Ripping a small strip from the bottom of my torn jacket, I tied my hair into a ponytail. Mother's worried face came to mind. What would happen to us after Gao told his father about today?

Since Father's arrest, I hadn't walked down Big Liberation Road. Mother said it wasn't safe. The Red Guards had split into two gangs, the Rights and the Lefts, who constantly fought each other. When Mother and I went out, we stayed on the back roads. But today, after the fight at school, nothing frightened me. The next time they ganged up on me, I might not be able to get away, but I decided I would at least get in a few punches and draw blood.

Someone shouted, "Get away! Get out of the way!" Rickshaws and bicycles crowded up onto the narrow sidewalk. A few people fell off their bicycles. I dashed aside to avoid being crushed. A green police jeep with a red flag roared by. A young worker with a paint-spattered uniform cursed at the jeep before getting back on his bike.

Like those around me, I elbowed my way into the

crowd. Father always had me walk closely behind him when we were in a crowd while he did the "elbow swimming."

The city jail stood one block from the department store. It was the only building with thick iron bars outside its windows. Two soldiers armed with machine guns guarded the iron gates. A group of people stood quietly outside the entrance, each hugging a small cloth bag. I envied them for knowing that their family member was inside. Day and night I wondered where they had taken my father.

Half a block from the jail was the bookstore. A huge portrait of Mao hung from the second floor of the building. He smiled and waved his big hand.

"Stop! Stop, or we'll kill you!" The voices came from behind me.

I froze. People around me parted.

Two Red Guards ran past me, closely chased by four more.

I jumped behind a big tree trunk.

About twenty yards away, the four caught up with the two.

"The Rights are going to beat up the Lefts this time," said a skinny young woman in a green post office uniform.

"What's the difference?" asked a middle-aged woman with gray hair. "Aren't they all Red Guards?"

"Oh, who knows. Each side thinks they follow Chairman Mao closer than the other. See how they wear their armbands?" The young woman moved closer to the fight. Some people on the sidewalk hurried on without looking; others watched from a distance.

The two Red Guards, who wore red armbands on their left arms, began swinging their belts. As they cut the air, the metal clasps and buckles made angry buzzing sounds. The four with red bands on their right arms backed off a few steps. I recognized Short Legs and Pimple Face among them.

Suddenly there was a sound like a cleaver hitting a slab of raw beef. Short Legs gave out a loud scream. Blood spurted from above his eye. The two Lefts broke from the circle and ran past the bookstore. Pimple Face and two other Rights chased them for a few steps and then ran back to Short Legs. "We will get them later!" Pimple Face gasped.

He lifted up Short Legs from behind. The other two carried his legs. They ran toward the hospital. As they passed me, I saw that Short Legs's face was covered with blood and his eyes were closed. A few kids followed behind. The crowd slowly broke up.

I had never seen a metal buckle crack open a head. How many stitches would it take to sew him up? Maybe he would die.

I would not be sorry if that happened. It had been seventeen months since they took Father away, but it still felt as recent as yesterday.

Something lay on the ground. It was the belt, the heavy buckle stained red. I hesitated, then walked over, picked it up, and tucked it into my schoolbag.

Tomorrow—tomorrow at school, if they humiliated me again, they would find out how far I would go to protect myself.

I zigzagged between people and bicycles toward Six-Port Revolutionary Road, which led to the Han River. The sun glowed on the sandy shore. I walked down the stone steps to the riverbank. A tugboat was pulling a huge barge loaded with lumber across the river. Birds sang in nearby trees. I plopped down where I used to sit with Father. Cupping my chin in my hands, I watched the river flow by. My mind flew in all directions.

Where was Father? Was it painful to drown oneself? When a person dies, does the spirit go to paradise? If so, was the Golden Gate Bridge along the way? No, no! I chased that thought away. I wanted to wear a red dress, eat ice cream, and walk on a green lawn. I wanted to live, to live for the day I could go to the Golden Gate Bridge with Father. But was he still alive? My eyes stung. I squeezed them shut.

The breeze became cooler as the day grew dark. My stomach groaned when I caught the scents of garlic fish and jasmine rice rising from the small boats. Mother should have left for her night shift by now. I walked toward home. Cars honked as they glided down Big Liberation Road. A full moon lit the busy sidewalk.

From inside our courtyard, I saw dim light flickering through our window. Mother was still home? I tiptoed upstairs and took a deep breath before cracking open the door.

A small oil lamp stood lit on the dinner table.

Mother sat on a low stool next to it, both hands wrapped around her knees. She stared into the darkness outside the window, looking small and helpless.

She didn't notice me until I walked over and touched her shoulder gently. "Momma, I'm home."

She looked up, her eyes red and puffy. "Do you know what you have done, Ling?"

"He called Father an American spy." I was too proud to tell her that Gao had spit on my face.

"But, Ling, don't you know who that boy's father is, and what he can do to us?" Mother paused. "They accused me of sending you to murder a young revolutionary." Mother rose from the stool. "Either you apologize or they'll make an example of us." She walked to where her nurse's uniform hung behind the door.

Anger burned inside me. I squeezed out each word between my teeth. "Apologize? No! Never!"

With her white uniform in hand, Mother turned toward me. "I know what they've been doing to you at school. You haven't done anything wrong. But I can't take it anymore—the fear, not knowing what happened to your father, and watching you suffer. I wish you would just bend a little, like a bamboo in the wind. If they send us to a labor camp, we will be treated worse than animals."

Words choked in my throat. Mother sighed and walked out. I ran to the window in my bedroom and watched her drag her skinny body through the courtyard. For a moment, I pictured myself apologizing to Gao. But the thought of his ugly face wearing a victory smile made me decide that I would rather die.

I sat down on my bed and took the belt out of my bag. Using a corner of my shirt, I buffed off the dark blood. With each stroke I felt more determined to fight.

My thoughts drifted from my fights with Gao at school to the baby doctor underneath the blue sheet and finally to the rope that had been under Mother's mattress. What would they do to Mother and me if I refused to apologize?

At last, my eyelids grew heavy. I collapsed into bed. I prayed that a fairy godmother would take me to the Golden Gate Bridge. More than anything else, I prayed that she could bring Father home safely.

But that night, I didn't dream.

Waiting for Daddy

To my surprise, Gao wasn't at school the next day or for several days after that. Yu and her gang whispered around me like annoying insects waiting for an opportunity to attack. Had I really injured Gao? If so, why hadn't I heard from his father? I tensed up each time a stranger walked into our classroom.

Since Teacher Hui's disappearance, visitors from the countryside, the army, and various factories came to our classroom every day. They lectured about the importance of class struggle, the misery of the old China, and their happiness in the new paradise China. When I listened, questions filled my head.

One chubby woman with a sour face came often. She talked about how Chairman Mao had made her life a thousand times better. Frowning down at my patched blue jacket and socks, now poking out the bottoms of my shoes, I thought she must be one of the few survivors from old China. Had she lost her father? Did she fight in the market for food or shop at the back door like Comrade Sin?

Father had always told me that knowledge was the most important thing in life. Was class struggle an excuse to punish good people? I felt frustrated that I had no one to whom I could ask my questions.

For the next few days, the weather stayed hot. Cicadas buzzed continuously. Gardener Zong's dog sat under the big milk tree with his tongue hanging out inches long. The heat added to my anxiety as I waited for Gao's revenge.

One night, Mother woke me. The air was muggy, and the bamboo mat stuck to my shirt.

"Do we need to go to the market?" I mumbled, rubbing my eyes. The only other reason I thought Mother would wake me was if Gao's father had finally come to take me away.

"No." Mother handed me my clothes. "Hurry. Your father is at the surgery ward!"

My eyes snapped open.

"Is he all right?" I jumped out of bed. This was the first news about Father since they had taken him away.

"He's operating on Comrade Sin."

I quickly pulled on my skirt. My toes hunted under the bed for my shoes. "Why is he operating on stupid Gao's father? Will they let him come home after that?"

"I don't know. No questions. Hurry!" Mother rushed out the door.

"What time is it?" I asked, following closely.

Mother put a finger in front of her lips and glanced at Comrade Li's door. As we hurried down the stairs, I tried to keep my plastic slippers from flapping. Feeling dizzy, I reached for the rail, which was still warm from the day's heat.

The burning pavement drilled through my plastic sandals. We tiptoed across the empty courtyard. The moon shone brightly between thick white clouds that swam across the sky. Mother slipped through the air in front of me. In her white cap and robe she reminded me of a ghost from old Chinese stories.

When we reached the hospital gate, Mother stopped.

"I have to go back before they notice I'm missing," she whispered.

"You can't come?" I knew how much she missed Father.

She shook her head. "Hide near the gate of the surgery ward. Take a good look at your father but don't talk to him; it'll cause trouble." Mother made a left turn and dashed toward the emergency room.

I sneaked straight ahead, following the long outdoor pathway that led to the two-story surgery ward, surrounded by a high brick wall. The air was hot against my face. There wasn't even a slight breeze.

A bright streetlight stood over the entrance. As I approached the open iron gate, bugs batted against my face. I slunk past the gate and into the shadow of a magnolia tree. Its big white flowers gave out a sweet fragrance. Broken stone tables and benches were piled up along the short walkway leading to the building. At one time they were nestled among lush bushes and flowering trees in the garden. The building was mostly dark, except for the waiting room at one end of the first floor and two surgery rooms on the second floor. Shadows moved behind curtains.

My heart drummed with happiness. One of the shadows was surely Father! Would he recognize me?

I was about to walk closer to the building when two light beams pointed at the gate. I crouched down behind the tree just in time.

A police jeep with a red flag hanging on the back pole stopped in front of the gate. Its horn honked twice. Were the police here because of Father? My hands turned clammy. Two men came out of the surgery ward. I held my breath and hoped one of them was Father.

"Hello, comrades!"

The high-pitched voice from the jeep belonged to Comrade Li! I had no chance of seeing Father if Comrade Li was here.

The two men from the ward strode into the light. They wore white shirts and baggy blue pants. One was tall and chopstick-skinny; the other was short with a big, round belly.

Comrade Li jumped out of the jeep and walked toward the men with his hands clasped behind his back. "Do you have a smoke?" His white shirt was unbuttoned.

Belly walked up to the gate and pulled out a pack of cigarettes. He lit one, took a puff, then passed it to Comrade Li. The cigarette gave off a choking smell. I swallowed to stifle a cough.

"What's happening in there?" Comrade Li pointed at the building with his cigarette.

"Chang is almost finished with Comrade Sin," said Chopstick. "But we wanted him to stay for a while longer to patch up a bunch of Rights. They were ambushed by some Lefts and are cut up pretty bad."

Comrade Li grunted. The glowing tip of his cigarette bobbed as he nodded his head.

My breaths grew rapid. Father was really here! In a sharp voice, Belly asked, "So, Comrade Sin is in bad shape?"

"Oh, yes," said Comrade Li. "He's been sick for some time. But he felt better today and called me over to have a drink."

"What happened then?" asked Chopstick.

"After we ate a few ribs and drank some sorghum wine, he started to throw up blood. I rushed him right over. That's why I called you to get Chang here from the jail."

Sweat tickled my forehead. I was afraid to lift my hand to wipe it off. I tried to make sense of what they were saying. Was that why Gao hadn't been in school, because of his sick father? They could bring Father here so quickly since they were keeping him in the city jail on Big Liberation Road. I couldn't wait to tell Mother.

Comrade Li let out a loud sigh. Smoke drifted around him. "I could have eaten more of those ribs. . . ."

Ribs! Despite my fear, my mouth watered. How I missed Mother's sweet garlic ribs!

"What about the Barefoot Doctors? Couldn't they have taken care of something like this?" asked Chopstick.

Father had talked about the Barefoot Doctors. They were young peasants with only eight weeks of medical training. Chairman Mao used them to replace the doctors he'd killed or sent to labor camps. They were known for their loyalty to the Revolution but also for making mistakes, like leaving surgical equipment inside patients.

Comrade Li took a puff on his cigarette. "I thought so. But Comrade Sin insisted that Barefoot Doctors are not ready for things like this. He wanted only Chang to operate on him. He kept saying, 'That's why we keep Chang nearby, in case a party member needs to be treated.'"

"After Chang fixes him, don't forget us when you go drinking," said Belly.

"Yes, yes!" Comrade Li interrupted. "Stay here and guard the building. I need your jeep a bit longer. I am going to get more to eat. Let Chang work on the Rights. When I return, take him back to the jail." Comrade Li climbed into the jeep and started the engine, grinding the gears. The tires squealed and released a burned-rubber smell as the jeep lurched down the road.

They were going to put Father back in jail after he saved Gao's father's life. Shouldn't they be thankful? Why did the police let Comrade Li boss them around? Was it because he was a friend of Jiang Qing? Would Mao let Barefoot Doctors treat him? Or maybe he never got sick.

Chopstick swatted at insects attracted by the light. "Bloodsucking bugs! Worse than the bourgeois!" *Slap. Slap.*

Belly laughed. "We are better off out here than inside. It's an oven in there." He took out his cigarette pack and walked outside the gate. Chopstick followed. Soon small clouds of smoke rose above their heads.

I decided to sneak around to the back of the ward and see if I could get up to the second floor. Staying in the shadows, I moved close to the building.

Above me, one lit window stood open without curtains. I saw no one inside, only tall shelves. It was the changing room, where the nurses and doctors dressed and washed their hands for surgery. I used to hide behind the shelves and surprise Father as he came out of surgery. I decided to climb in and wait for Father there.

I crept toward the back end of the ward, where a narrow iron staircase led to the second floor. Doctors and nurses used it to come down to the garden on their breaks.

Trash piled around the stairs stunk of rotting vegetables and rice. In the moonlight, scraps of newspaper, empty cans, and half-torn garbage bags looked like they'd been covered with a coat of frosting. I held the back of my hand in front of my nose and breathed between my fingers. Sweat plastered my clothes against my body. My feet became slippery in my plastic sandals. I took them off and tucked them in the back waistband of my skirt before stepping on the staircase.

When I grabbed the rail, something stuck to my fingers. It felt like a banana peel. I was between the first and second floor when something cold splashed on my head. Blinded, I couldn't help but give out a shriek.

"Who is there?" a man's voice cried out above me. "Hurry! Lefts! The Lefts are here!"

I wiped my eyes with the back of my wrist. Soggy limp tea leaves stuck to me like leeches. Scrambling down the stairs, I ran toward the bushes near the courtyard wall. Two hands grabbed me from behind and threw me to the ground. Chopstick pulled me up and held my arms.

"Who are you with? What are you doing here?"

His raspy voice echoed in my ears. I struggled to free myself from his iron grip. He slapped my face with his greasy hand.

My ears rang and I felt a knot in my throat. Inside I wept, *Daddy, please come out now.*

"She can't be with the Lefts." Belly laughed. "She's too young."

Chopstick twisted my arms behind me. "Get inside!" He pushed me into the building.

Without long lines of patients waiting in the hallway, the surgery ward seemed much larger. I heard moaning before Chopstick pushed me into the waiting room.

Bright bulbs dangled from bare wires. Two long benches in the middle of the room were crowded with wounded Red Guards. Blood oozed from all parts of their bodies. The stink of sweat and a metallic smell filled the steamy room. The walls began to swim before my eyes. I leaned against the dirty wooden door.

Two doctors in white uniforms squatted before a Red Guard slumped at the end of one bench, studying a knife stuck in his leg. His left forearm covered his eyes. A cream-colored pail holding a roll of bandages and a few cotton balls sat next to them on the floor.

"You sure it's a good idea?" asked a round-faced doctor with a broken front tooth. "If you pull it out, he may bleed to death."

"What else do you suggest?" asked the other. "He can't live the rest of his life with a knife in his leg." Their countryside accent told me they were Barefoot Doctors.

The Red Guard stirred and spoke. "Leave it alone. Let Chang deal with it." The doctors looked at each other and stood up.

That voice! I had not heard it in a long time, but I was sure it was Niu. Despite the heat, a chill gripped me. Would he die from bleeding? I bit my lip and stared at his leg. Blood oozed onto his shoe, staining it dark red.

Chopstick turned to the crowd. "Anyone know this girl?" He let go of my arm.

The doctors stopped arguing. Niu raised his hand and our eyes met. His face was pale, his eyes full of pain. I held my breath.

"Anyone know her?" repeated Chopstick.

If he told them who I was, it would bring more trouble to Father.

Niu closed his eyes.

At that moment, I realized I could no longer hate him so much.

"Don't waste time with her. Lock her up," said Belly. "Let Comrade Li deal with her in the morning."

"Come with me, then!" Chopstick pinched my ear and dragged me to the opposite end of the surgery ward. He let go of my burning ear and opened the last door. As he pushed me through the doorway, I tripped and landed on something soft. Moonlight splashed in through a high, grimy window. I was lying on a filthy mattress. The reek of mold and other foul odors stirred my empty stomach. Chopstick spat on the mattress, closed the door, and locked it from the outside.

Stacks of stained, smelly mattresses surrounded me. Mosquitoes and other bugs hummed about, attacking my nose, arms, and legs. I stood up and batted at them. Soon, I was too tired to fight. Stepping onto the stack below the window, I noticed the glass was broken. A grille of long iron bars locked me in. Through the bars, I could see the pathway that led to the main gate. All was quiet except for faint voices and footsteps from other parts of the building.

If I stayed awake, I could see Father when he left the building. I hoped he could remove the knife from

Niu's leg soon. The pain on his face and the image of his bleeding leg made me feel sorry for him. Did he regret what he had done to us?

Crickets sang short tunes in the courtyard, with three beats between each round. It grew tiring to my ears. I wished Father would walk out of the building now. But with all the wounded Red Guards, it could take hours. I sat down on one of the mattresses and struggled to keep my eyes open.

A bumping noise from outside the door awakened me. Gardener Zong came in dragging a dirty mattress. His white T-shirt was soiled yellow, and his black shorts were secured above his hips with a belt made of long cloth bandages. Beads of sweat hung on his flat nose and round cheeks. When he saw me, his eyebrows shot up.

"What are you doing here, Ling? Your mother is worried to death about you!"

I was glad to see his friendly face. I knew I could trust him. Busy street noises came from outside. My eyes ached from the sunlight glaring through the window. Thirsty and hot, I struggled to get up. My hair clung to the mattress. "Is my father still upstairs?"

"Oh, no. They took him back to jail hours ago." Gardener Zong laid the mattress on one of the stacks. "Go home, Ling. Now!" He waved his hand toward the door.

How could I have fallen asleep! If I had stayed at the window, I wouldn't have missed him. But I did have some good news; I couldn't wait to tell Mother they kept Father close by.

The hallway was now filled with moaning patients waiting in lines. I ran past a nurse, who pushed a squeaky wheelchair toward me. In it sat an old man folding his hands over his stomach, groaning. Empty soda bottles, smashed cigarette packs, and fruit peels were scattered on the floor. I took shallow breaths as I made my way out of the surgery ward and back to the street. A blue truck loaded with watermelons passed by, throwing up a cloud of dust. I felt dizzy in the hot sun, and my body itched as if thousands of ants crawled over me, especially my scalp. I ran as fast as I could but had to stop often to scratch my legs. They were covered with red bites.

Mother and I met at the doorway.

"What happened, my dear?" Mother threw her arms around me. The back of her blue shirt was damp with sweat. I wanted to enjoy this real hug from her, but I was too itchy. I freed my hands to scratch.

"I didn't get to see Father, but I know where—"

"Oh, dear, what's in your hair?" Mother took a step back from me. "Lice! Ling, you have lice." She dragged me close to the window and into the sunlight. "Yes, it's lice."

Howling Wolf

Mother picked up a stack of old newspapers from beside the stove. Carefully, she checked every page before laying it around a stool, setting two sheets with Chairman Mao's pictures on the counter. Months earlier, a nurse had been sent to prison as an anti-Maoist just because she lit her stove with a newspaper page with Mao's photo on it.

I noticed a cloth rice sack in the corner next to some herbal medicine bottles, and folded clothes. "Why are you packing, Mom?"

"When they come for us, I want to be ready." She led me to the stool and raked her hard-toothed comb through my hair.

As each stroke yanked my hair, pain shot through my lice-chewed scalp. I clenched my teeth, not wanting to cry out. Were we going to a labor camp?

Before knowing that they kept Father in the jail nearby, I had wished they would send us to his camp, wherever it was. Now I didn't want to leave. I wanted to be here in case they ever brought him back to the hospital.

Something cold drizzled through my hair. Within a second, my scalp burned. "I hope this will kill the lice," Mother whispered. Her ox-bone comb scraped against my raw scalp.

I couldn't endure any more of the pain and the itching. "You are hurting me!" I shouted.

Mother stopped.

Stiffening my back, I waited for her to scold me for raising my voice and showing disrespect.

A moment later, she whispered, "Ling, your hair is too thick. The coal oil can't kill all the lice." She put down her comb and left the room.

Hadn't she heard me shouting? What was she planning to do now?

Mother returned with a pair of scissors and Father's razor. "We have to shave your head."

I jumped off the chair. "No! There must be another way."

She took a step back. "I don't know what else to do, Ling. I used up this month's ration. I even emptied the lamp. If I don't cut your hair, the lice will spread throughout the apartment." She tilted the blue oil cup, showing me it was empty. We received two cups of coal oil each month. Without the oil, we'd have to live in the dark for the rest of the month. I hated myself for being caught and for falling asleep on the dirty mattress.

Seeing sadness in her eyes, I knew she wouldn't cut my hair if she could find another way. As far back as I could remember, she had told me that ladies should let their hair grow.

"Do what you must!" I was shaking, trying to hold my despair inside. I threw myself back into the chair. I didn't care about being a lady. I wanted to be a mean dragon. More than anything, I wanted to stop the pain and itching. I thought of Jiang Qing's ugly short hair.

Digging my nails into my thighs, I fixed my eyes on Mao's smiling portrait. *Are you happy that I'm suffering?*

Mother took hold of a clump of my hair. I waited

for the dreadful sound of cutting. Nothing happened. I turned and looked at her. The tears in her eyes spoke words that she could not.

I couldn't bear to see her cry. This had to be done. Taking the scissors from her, I cut a lock of my hair on the side, close to my scalp. The long hair dropped on my legs, then landed on the newspapers. Glancing again at the rice sack, I told myself I'd have no need for hair in the labor camp.

Mother wiped her arm roughly against her face, smearing a short, dark streak of tears across her cheek. Taking the scissors from me, she cut the rest of my hair. Locks piled around me on the newspapers. I thought of Mrs. Wong's hair falling on the leaves.

When there was no long hair left to cut, she picked up Father's razor. As she shaved my head, I felt the drops of her tears raining on my scalp. I was trying hard not to cry out, but my own eyes had welled up like a dam about to burst.

After shaving my head, Mother emptied all three hot water thermoses into the wooden tub. Unlike other times, she set a new bar of soap on top of the scraps in the chipped bowl. Did she feel sorry for me? I used up half that bar scrubbing myself, cherishing the privilege. I stayed in the tub until the water turned cold and gray. By the time I got out, about twenty white lice floated on the surface. A couple seemed to swim toward me. Disgusted, I quickly turned away.

Looking into the small mirror on the wall, I remembered a patched doll I once saw. I stared at a stranger with bloodshot eyes and a goose-egg head covered with scrapes and red bumps. I used to think Jiang Qing was ugly, but at least she had hair. Now I believed anyone who saw me must think I was either an ugly boy or a mental patient.

I thought of the crazy lady who walked around our school telling anyone willing to listen that the Red Guards took her son to meet Chairman Mao. Gao and his gang often followed and threw rocks at her. They yelled that her son was dead. But when she stuck her two pinkies in her mouth, pulled her lips apart, and yowled like a wolf, they ran like scared dogs.

I stuck my pinkies in my mouth, pulled, and

howled at the mirror. Mine wasn't as scary as hers. I would get better with practice.

Mother ran in. "Are you all right? What was that noise?"

I answered her with a wolf smile.

I had already missed the morning lecture. As much as I hated school, I knew better than to miss the afternoon political studies. Would my enemies at school be surprised to see my shaved head after I fought with them over cutting my braids? My body tensed as I thought of their faces lighting up with laughter.

I grabbed my schoolbag, and Mother handed me a cold steamed bun. "Please don't get into more trouble."

I didn't want to upset her, but I could not promise anything. I avoided her stare as I walked past her out the door.

The hot September sun scorched my shaven head as I walked down the alley. Itching all over, my head felt like it was stuffed with sticky rice glue. I felt a twinge of pain in my chest and my ears throbbed.

I bit into the bun. It tasted like plaster. The surge of nausea came and I ran to the side of the street. I heaved again and again, but I couldn't bring anything up.

From a block away, two women stopped and stared at me. I wasn't sure if it was because of my shaved head or the horrible retching sounds I made. I forced myself to continue walking.

Noise from classrooms spilled out into the school courtyard. Gao and his gang stood in a knot inside the classroom window. For a moment, I wanted to turn and walk away. But then I thought, *I can't hide forever. I must show them I'm not afraid.* I pulled the belt out of my bag. Lifting up my baggy blue shirt, I wrapped it around my waist, then clasped the cold metal buckle against my stomach. It gave me confidence and strength. Now I was ready for political studies.

The bell for the afternoon session had faded away by the time I entered the classroom. Gao stood in front of the class, behind the teacher's desk. Our eyes locked in hate. This was the first time I had seen him since our fight. His oversized Mao's hat made his pudgy face look small. The rest of the class remained at their desks, eyes fixed on me from all directions. Whispers buzzed around me like flies. I planned my strategy as I walked toward my seat near the rear window. If they attacked again, I could escape through the back door or jump out the window. Yet I would not let them drive me out easily.

Holding my head high, I glanced around. Whenever my eyes met theirs, they turned away.

Perhaps with my bald head, they didn't know who I was, or they thought I had gone mad. I made my wolf smile at Gao. He ignored me and continued flipping through his red book.

I leaned back in my chair and pulled out my red book, waiting for my name to be called. Occasionally I could hear the math teacher's hoarse voice from upstairs. It must be his turn to read for the teachers' political studies. Outside, a little breeze stirred the leaves. Cicadas took a break in their song. A black cat sat on the windowsill for a minute, then jumped away.

As usual, Gao called on students one by one. He always assigned the long, hard passages for me to read. Even if I recited them flawlessly, he made up reasons to criticize me.

The day before our fight, he had assigned me to read Chairman Mao's "Classes and Class Struggles." As I was reading he had rudely interrupted me.

"Stop, you bourgeois bug!" He waved his hand. "Your voice showed no love to dear Chairman Mao."

I swallowed my angry words, for again I remembered Mother pleading, "Ling, we can't afford any more trouble."

Now Gao took his turn, reading "On Youth." I tried hard not to laugh as he chanted slowly, his voice climbing to a high pitch, like a whining cat.

Next, Gao had Yu read "Kill the bourgeois bugs! Save the patient!" It was Gao's favorite, but he never read it himself. Perhaps there were too many words in it that he couldn't pronounce. I wondered if Mao knew he shouldn't kill all the bugs. Father had told me that some bugs were good for people.

I followed the study session with half an ear. A pair of yellow butterflies danced outside the window near me. In the distance, a helicopter's rotor ticked faintly. I propped up Mao's book on the desk, folded my arms, and rested my head. I hoped that from the front of the classroom it still appeared as if I was reading along. By now I had lost track of the page Yu was reading. The first cool breeze in weeks came through the window, soothing my itchy body. It smelled of chrysanthemums. My mind flew thousands of miles away. Father had told me the air was always cool around the Golden Gate Bridge. My eyes slid shut.

Father and I walked along the Golden Gate Bridge. I counted ships as they passed below. The fog lifted at the far end of the bridge. A little girl in a red dress walked toward me. Behind her were colorful houses with green lawns. This must be paradise. I turned to tell Father, but he was gone. Someone was calling my name.

"Ling, Ling. . . ."

I jerked awake.

"Ling!" Gao yelled. "Your turn, Bald Head!"

The class broke into laughter.

I had no idea what I was supposed to read.

Whispers came around. "'On Youth.' 'On Youth.'"

I thought Gao had just read that. Why would some-one help me? Was this a trap? With no better choice, I blinked in surprise and quickly turned to the page.

I read as fast as I could, expecting Gao to stop me at any time because I didn't sound like a whining cat.

> *The world is yours,*
> *As well as ours,*
> *But in the last analysis, it is yours.*

Underneath the desk, I clenched my fist and kneaded my aching stomach.

> *You young people,*
> *Full of vigor and vitality,*
> *Are in the bloom of life,*
> *Like the sun at eight or nine in the morning.*
> *Our hope is placed on you.*

Gao's hand crashed down on the teacher's desk. "Stop! Daughter of the spy, you dare fall asleep during political studies?" he shouted. The visor of his hat slid to the side, covering his left ear.

It was a trap! I was reading the wrong passage.

As Gao stalked toward me I tensed, ready to leap from my desk. I undid the belt buckle under the table.

Clang! Clang! the school bell rang out. The PA system hummed to life. Everyone looked around in confusion; it was never used during political studies.

"Attention, comrades!" A woman announcer paused, sobbing. "With deep regret, we have to inform you that our beloved leader, Chairman Mao, died last night on September 9, 1976, at the age of eighty-two." She wept again. Then the PA cut off. The news blasted inside me. I tried to keep still, but my heart felt like a bird about to be freed from its cage. I knew he was old, but every day millions of people shouted "Long live Chairman Mao!" I had thought he'd never die. Something wild leapt in my heart. Father!

My classmates shuffled out, murmuring and weeping. Gao stood frozen in front of my desk and hunched over, as if someone had punched him in the stomach. Soon, we were the only two left in the classroom. With one hand still holding the belt, I used the other hand to stuff Mao's red book into my schoolbag.

Gao waved his clenched fist in front of my face and shouted, "I will kill you soon, bourgeois bug." My naked scalp tightened and anger surged in me. Drawing the belt from under my shirt, I stood and whipped the buckle down on the desk between us. Bits of wood flew off the desk. I wanted to show him I was not a bug, but a fearless dragon.

Gao jumped back.

"Stay away from me or I will put you in the hospital right next to your father." What I really wanted was to put him in a coffin next to Mao. With my back straight, I marched past him as he stood like a dead tree stump, his mouth hanging open, showing his rotting teeth.

Pig Fat

For six weeks, the loudspeakers around the city bellowed funeral music.

My life with Mother hadn't changed as I'd hoped. We got no more news about Father or the Wongs, and I still hadn't seen any ribs.

Coming home for lunch one afternoon, I smelled the scent of frying pig fat from our window. My mouth watered. I ran up the stairs two steps at a time.

Someone with a crutch under his left arm stood outside our door. He turned to face me. It was Niu. The two lower buttons of his blue jacket were missing. I hadn't stood this close to him since the night he arrested Father. He was taller, and his skin darker. A thin, weedy mustache appeared above his lips. Words choked in my throat.

"Here!" He held out a white shirt. "It needs mending."

It appeared to be one of Father's shirts. "How did you get this?" I grabbed it from him.

Without answering, he turned and hobbled past me. I watched until his back disappeared down the stairs. I pressed the shirt close to my nose. It smelled like Father and the hospital.

"Who's there?" Mother stepped out of the apartment.

I handed her the shirt. "Niu gave me this," I whispered. Her eyes widened, and her mouth opened a little.

She glanced toward Comrade Li's door. It was closed. We hadn't seen much of him since Mao's death. When he did come home, he sang like a drunken sailor, filling the hallway with the pungent smell of rice wine. Mother pushed me inside and closed the door. I followed her to the kitchen.

Sitting on two low stools near the stove, we examined the yellowed shirt. It had neatly stitched patches on both elbows.

"Look at this, Mom." I pointed to a patch under the armpit. It had bigger stitches.

"Your father is better at mending patients than shirts." Mother tried to rip out the thread, but it was too strong. "He used surgical thread. This must be what he wants mended." She broke the thread with her teeth. Three layers of old hospital sheet peeled off.

My heart raced with excitement. On the inside piece, in perfectly horizontal rows, were characters as small as ants written in blue fountain-pen ink. I grabbed the cloth and read quickly.

> *I am healthy, getting enough to eat. They let me treat prisoners and guards. Sell my watch to buy food.*
> *Love and miss you both!*

The last words were smudged. Tears from Father? My throat tightened. Had Father given Niu the shirt while he was treating him in the hospital? If so, how did Father know he could trust him? Tears ran down Mother's face. Even though it was the only valuable item left in our home, Mother never had sold Father's watch. I had seen her holding it many times, but she always put it back in the rice jar, its hiding place.

I reached out and hugged her. Mother stroked my head, as though she were rubbing memories back into me. I became very still. Her herbal medicine had long since healed the bites and scratches under my inch-long hair. And then her hand dropped and she stood up.

"Come help me." She went over to the corner under the window, picked up a few pieces of coal shaped like Ping-Pong balls, and dropped them inside the slow-burning stove. It wasn't until now that I noticed the small white pieces of half-cooked pig fat in the wok. Four bottles of herbal medicine sat around the stove.

"What are these for?" I asked.

"Gardener Zong told me this morning that your father will be operating on Comrade Sin again." Mother sat down on the short stool next to the stove. "He offered to take something to him." She put the wok on the stove.

I squatted next to her. "Did Gardener Zong tell you when?" I needed a plan. This time I would make sure they did not catch me.

Mother narrowed her eyes and looked at me suspiciously. "No, he didn't. Ling, don't do anything that will get us into more trouble." She pressed the pig fat with a metal spatula. Oil spurted from beneath it.

"Why does Comrade Sin need another operation? Is he drinking again?" The way Gao treated me made me wish his father would never get better.

"No, he is bleeding inside. In his last operation, two Barefoot Doctors sewed him up while your father went to treat injured Red Guards."

"Did they leave a scalpel inside him? Is he going to die, like Mao?" I asked hopefully.

Mother glared. "Don't talk like that. Your father can fix him."

"Why?" I couldn't help but raise my voice. "Why does Father have to treat them? After what they have done to us, how can he forgive them?"

Mother stopped pressing the pig fat; her face turned serious. "Your father believes that a true doctor will treat each patient with care, even his enemy."

I thought of the hidden calligraphy of the Physician's Creed. Did the person who wrote it ever have to go to jail? If so, would he still think a great physician should treat his enemy with compassion? I wasn't sure I could treat my enemy with care. I had imagined many different ways for Gao to suffer and die.

"Hurry! Empty the cough medicine into the big bowl. I have to deliver this to Gardener Zong before Aunt Wu comes for her acupuncture treatment."

"What are you going to do with it?" I opened the plastic cover on the glass bottle.

"I'm rendering the lard for your father. If we mix the oil with it and then make them into balls, it will look and smell like herbal medicine. Hopefully the guards won't take it."

The medicine was a dark brown mixture of herbs and honey. When I had craved sweets, I used to spread it like jam on steamed bread. One time, I ate too much and had diarrhea for three days. I stirred the thick mixture with two chopsticks to loosen it and then poured it into the bowl.

I stared at the curling pig fat, now shrunken and crispy brown. The smell hung in the air just beyond reach of my tongue. How delicious it would taste with salt sprinkled on top! I longed to have just one small piece. But Father needed the lard to help him stay strong. I swallowed hard.

"What's happening at school?" Mother asked.

"We're still crying for Mao." My eyes were fixed on the iron wok.

Mother sighed.

To show our love for Chairman Mao, we had to cry for one hour in the morning and one hour in the afternoon. During an afternoon crying session, one boy from the fourth grade said he had no more tears left. The next day the police came and took him away.

It wasn't hard for me. I had many reasons to feel heartbroken. I made a list in my mind: on Monday I cried for Mrs. Wong; on Tuesday I cried for Father; on Wednesday I cried for my blouse; on Thursday I cried for my hair; on Friday I cried for the ribs I missed so much; on Saturday I cried for the hidden picture of the Golden Gate Bridge. When Sunday came, I was glad I didn't have to cry.

I had thought that Mao's death would change everything, especially when a month later, the new Central Government arrested Jiang Qing and her supporters. The new chairman had shocked the whole nation by accusing her and her gang of planning to overthrow the new government.

Aside from the crying, for me the only change was that I had become infamous among the two hundred students at school. They stared at my head, whispering loud enough for me to hear, "She's that crazy girl that almost killed Gao with her belt."

Living up to my reputation, I now wore the belt over my blue shirt. I never had to use it again though. The one time Gao's gang got close to me, all it took was a wolf scream and they backed away. I was relieved that they no longer bothered me but in my heart I felt lonely. I wished someone would talk to me, even to pick a fight.

Mother handed me a wooden spoon. "Keep stirring while I add the oil." With the front part of her jacket, she lifted the wok by the handles, tilted it slightly, and slowly drizzled oil into the bowl.

As I stirred, the dark brown medicine became lighter. The mixture turned sticky as the oil cooled. My arm grew tired, but I didn't stop. It felt good to do something for Father.

Mother showed me how to roll the mixture into half-inch herbal medicine balls. Between each ball, she dipped her hands into a bowl of cold water to keep them from sticking.

When we finished, it was almost time for me to go to the afternoon crying session.

I hoped. I wished. But I was embarrassed to ask.

At last, Mother scooped up two spoonfuls of the rendered pig fat, put them into a bowl, and mixed in some rice. With two fingers, she reached into the salt jar, took out a pinch, and sprinkled it on top of the rice mixture. Stretching out my shaking hands, I took the bowl from her. "Thank you, Mom!"

It tasted heavenly! I fed the last spoonful into Mother's mouth before rushing out the door with my schoolbag. As I ran past Comrade Li's apartment, his door swung open. There he stood, smelling like a liquor jar.

"Bourgeois Sprout, where are you running to?" he shouted. His stained blue jacket was unbuttoned, showing his pale chest.

I showed him my afraid-of-nothing face, but inside I trembled. "School." I stared right in his eyes. I had never seen his Mao jacket this dirty and wrinkled.

"I smell meat cooking in your home." He took a deep sniff. "What are you celebrating?" Without waiting for an answer, he continued. "It's about time I took care of you two." He laughed, showing his corn-yellow teeth. His foul breath brushed my forehead.

I ran down to the courtyard. Outside, the wind had stopped and the sun hid behind thick clouds. The air was cool and dusty. All afternoon, I was anxious and fearful. Had Comrade Li expected Comrade Sin to punish us? With Comrade Sin still sick, had he decided to act on his own? Would he send us away or hold a public criticism meeting? If only I knew where he planned to send us, then I could ask Gardener Zong to tell Father. Or maybe I shouldn't. It would only worry Father.

Golden Gate Bridge

As I walked home from school that afternoon, I decided that if Comrade Li planned to send us away, I would talk Mother into hiding until we could find Father. But I wasn't sure who would dare take us in. My head hurt as I tried to remember friends we used to have and patients my parents had treated.

Inside our courtyard, a stage made from old tables sat in front of our building. I instantly broke out in a sweat. Today was the day I had feared for so long.

Comrade Li sat on the edge of the stage, smoking. Pimple Face, Short Legs, and Mouse Eyes gathered around him. Gao, Yu, and three other boys from my class huddled around a rectangular blackboard on the ground.

I walked toward them, forcing myself not to show fear, but my steps became shaky. I wasn't sure if I should run.

No wonder Gao wore a big grin and had whispered to his gang all afternoon. I sensed they were talking about me, but I had no way to know for sure. When the bell rang at the end of the school day, they'd raced out of the classroom.

Comrade Li saw me first. He pointed with his cigarette-yellowed finger. "There's the enemy. Go get her!" he called out shrilly.

All eyes turned to me. Gao and Yu jumped up. When my eyes met Gao's, he hesitated.

Pimple Face pushed him from behind. "Go! We are here to protect you."

As I reached for my belt, Gao screamed, "She is going to hit me!" and ran.

Short Legs and Mouse Eyes rushed to me, grabbed my arms, and twisted them back. Pain spread through my body as I kicked and cursed. Yu pushed Gao forward. He yanked my belt away without looking into my eyes. Together, they pushed me in front of Comrade Li. I could see a few greasy black sesame seeds stuck on his chin. I turned my face away from him. Comrade Li took a puff of his cigarette and blew smoke into my face. My throat felt like it was being scratched by fish bones, and I broke into a hacking cough.

"Take her onstage!" he barked.

Short Legs and Mouse Eyes dragged me up while Gao and Yu kicked and punched me from behind.

Uncrossing his legs, Comrade Li shouted through his loudspeaker. "Time for a meeting! Everyone! Report to the courtyard!"

I stopped struggling and stood in the middle of the stage. I looked toward our windows, hoping Mother was not home. Maybe she had gone to deliver the medicine balls to Gardener Zong. But I saw something move behind the kitchen curtain. It was Mother's gray hair. I gasped for breath and prayed she wouldn't come out.

Short Legs, Pimple Face, and Yu were behind me. Gao stood to my left, holding the blackboard with a loop of rope over one end. Now I saw the white characters on it: LING APOLOGIZES TO GAO!

Why should I apologize to him? His threat to cut off my hair or his accusing Father of being a spy?

The clouds shifted away to the east. The warm air brushed my face. About a dozen people— old men, women, and young children—dragged themselves out of neighboring buildings. They whispered among themselves. Others were still at work. Two middle-aged nurses who worked at night like Mother had just returned from shopping. One carried a wok and a spatula, the other swung a basketful of muddy vegetables. A little round-faced boy wanted to climb onto the stage, but his grandmother scooped him up. He started crying.

"Quiet! Quiet!" Comrade Li raised his free hand. "You are here today to witness a public apology. Ling, apologize to Gao now," ordered Comrade Li through the speaker.

"No," I snarled. "Never!"

He jumped onto the stage and grabbed the front of my jacket. "Apologize!" Comrade Li shouted, his foul breath blowing into my face.

"No!" I glared at him, remembering the baby doctor's brave son.

His hand came across my face, once, twice, and a third time. My cheeks stung, and I tasted blood in my mouth.

A surge of fear gripped me. I saw the image of the baby doctor's son rolling and bleeding on the ground.

The slapping finally stopped. "Gao, bring the board here." I opened my eyes. Comrade Li waved his hand. Wearing a big grin, Gao moved close to me, holding the board.

There, coming out of our building, was Mother. She staggered toward us, looking terrified. I shivered in the October sun.

If they saw her, they would turn on her, too. I did not feel one bit sorry for my fight with Gao, but I regretted putting Mother in danger. If they were going to punish someone, let it be just me.

"I apologize to Gao," I said weakly. I couldn't believe the words came out. Overwhelmed by shame, tears welled up. I forced them down and wished I had enough courage to take the belt from Gao and whip him to the ground. In truth, I was uncertain whether I could take more beating. Even more, I was scared of what they would do to Mother. I decided I must do anything to protect her.

"What?" Comrade Li sounded surprised.

"I apologize to Gao!" Raising my voice, I straightened up. Short Legs and Pimple Face loosened their grip, and they let go of my arms.

I turned to Gao, grabbed the board from him, and threw the rope over my head. "I will announce my apology to the whole hospital," I said loudly.

Silence fell.

I jumped off the stage and took the wok and spatula from the nurse standing in front. She looked surprised but didn't stop me. Rapping the wok with the spatula, I began to chant. *Bang!* "I apologize to Gao!" *Bang! For his stupidity.*

I had to distract them. I'd do anything, anything, to lead them away from Mother. That was the only way to keep her safe.

Bang! Bang! "I apologize to Gao!" *For his being so ugly.*

The board was heavier than I expected. The rope cut into the back of my neck through my black cotton sweater.

Gao and Yu giggled behind me.

As long as I am alive, I will seek revenge. Bang! "I apologize to Gao!"

A few children joined in my chant. Strangely, the shame became less overwhelming.

"Louder!" Gao barked, pushing me hard from behind.

I teetered. In the corner of my eye, I saw Aunt Wu dragging Mother toward our building.

Bang! Feeling relief, I raised my voice. "I apologize to Gao!"

Wearing an amused, wicked smile, Comrade Li walked along in measured steps.

A few drops of rain fell on my burning cheeks, which must have been swelling. Clouds now covered most of the sun.

As I walked through the front gate of the courtyard onto Victory Road, the bicycles and rickshaws halted to let me cross. I stopped chanting, embarrassed and rattled by all the people on the street with their eyes fastened on me. They whispered and pointed.

Gao kicked me and shouted, "Don't stop! Apologize to me!"

Bang! Bang! "I apologize to Gao!" *For his being born.*

My feet locked on the ground the moment I entered the hospital gate. A small crowd of doctors and nurses was already gathering inside. A big army truck parked beside them. My stomach churned when I recognized two of the six men in police uniforms who climbed out—Chopstick and Belly! I wished I had found a place for Mother and me to hide. How wrong I was to hope life would get better after Mao's death.

Comrade Li's smile faded for a moment and then returned. He pulled my ear from behind and said, "They have arrived for you at a good time!"

I shook my head forcefully, and my ear slipped from his fingers.

"After they haul you away," he said with a shrewd smile, "it will be your mother's turn. She will have to confess that she ordered you to kill this loyal Young Pioneer." He patted Gao's shoulder.

Despair overcame me. All my pain and humiliation had been for nothing. It had been foolish to think Comrade Li would forget about Mother. I thought about attacking Comrade Li with the spatula. As if reading my mind, Pimple Face yanked the wok and spatula out of my hands.

"Hello, comrades!" Comrade Li screeched. "Here is your little bourgeois prisoner." He pushed me forward, almost bumping me into Chopstick. I struggled to stay upright and dug my fingers into the edge of the shameful blackboard.

Standing there like a bee bound in a spiderweb, I knew it was no use to run.

Chopstick pushed me aside.

"No. We are here for you!" Belly jabbed at Comrade Li's chest with a baton, baring his broad teeth. "You are under arrest for being in Jiang Qing's gang." He laughed with a gurgling sound from his throat.

I stumbled to the nearest wall to support myself. The crowd kept its distance, watching. Comrade Li screamed insults at Chopstick and tried to hit him with his loudspeaker. Chopstick stepped aside. With his baton, Belly knocked the loudspeaker to the ground.

"You think you are untouchable?" Chopstick punched Comrade Li in the face. Two streams of blood trickled from his nose.

"I am a real Maoist!" screamed Comrade Li. "You

can't treat me like this!" Bloody saliva flowed from his mouth. His face was as red as a rooster's comb, and his eyes shone with desperate tears. A large crowd formed around them.

"You're not a Maoist. You're just a little rotten shrimp in Jiang Qing's gang." Whistles and jeers from the crowd joined Chopstick's loud laughter.

What was the difference between a Maoist and Jiang Qing's gang? They had both helped Mao kill so many people. Did he hold the meeting today without Comrade Sin because he sensed his days were numbered? Could I dare hope this time that our lives might finally get better? But Father, where was my father?

Two policemen twisted Comrade Li's arms behind his back and handcuffed his wrists. Chopstick pushed Comrade Li's neck down, stretching his head so low, he probably saw only the yellow leaves on the ground. I removed the board from my neck. With my fingers, I drew an X through the chalk characters. Gao stared at me. I made a wolf face at him, and he looked away. Suddenly, he darted toward the truck parked next to the gate. In the back sat Comrade Sin, his head shaking back and forth with something stuffed in his mouth.

My head spun. They had arrested his father! So Gao had become an antirevolutionary, too. No one could make me apologize for hitting a People's Enemy. I pictured his crying face as the Young Pioneers ripped the red scarf from around his short neck.

They dragged Comrade Li back into the courtyard. Belly kicked the back of Comrade Li's knees with his army boot. Comrade Li stopped kicking and swinging from side to side. But he didn't stop yelling "You can't treat me like this! I love Chairman Mao!"

"Shut up! We have put Jiang Qing in jail, and now we can treat you any way we want," roared Chopstick, stuffing a dirty rag into Comrade Li's mouth. Everyone watched in silence. I couldn't tell if they were happy or surprised. The crowd grew larger.

Four men pulled Comrade Li onto the stage. The muscles in his face twitched as if a cockroach tickled inside his mouth. Had he ever expected a day like this? Too bad he didn't have long hair for me to cut.

Pimple Face started banging the wok with the spatula. As he circled the courtyard, he called out,

"Everyone to the courtyard!" *Bang!* "Witness the public trial!" *Bang!* "Of the Jiang Qing gang member!" Short Legs, Mouse Eyes, and Yu yelled along. "Witness the public trial!" *Bang!* "Jiang Qing gang!" *Bang!*

I couldn't believe how fast they had turned against Comrade Li.

As the crowd closed in around the stage, I searched for Mother. Why wasn't she here? Remembering the white rope under her bed, I ran upstairs to our home. As I reached for my key, the door flew open. I froze, afraid to blink, fearing that what I saw might disappear.

It was Father! He looked older and smaller than I remembered. Fish-tail wrinkles spread from the corners of his eyes toward his mostly gray hair. Yet he stood straight, head held high. The light in his eyes was just as I remembered.

I had dreamed of this moment, practicing a thousand times what I would say. Now all I could do was stare.

Father murmured something I couldn't quite hear.

My hands flew up to cover my aching cheeks. Realizing how grimy my fingers were, I hid them in the pockets of my baggy jacket. I wished I had a

Mao's hat to cover my shaved head. Was he surprised to see that his little girl now looked so ugly? The shouts, chants, and banging on the wok from the courtyard drowned out rolling thunder from a distant storm. I stood frozen. I had pictured crying at this moment, but where were my tears?

Father opened his arms. "Come here, my beautiful girl!" He wrapped his arms around me.

I buried my face in his shoulder. He smelled just as I remembered. Like a tightly rolled tea leaf dropped in hot water, I unfolded, feeling lighter by the second. Happy tears showered my face. Father's arms squeezed out all the sadness and suffering.

Outside, the sun pushed through the dark clouds.

Mother stood next to us, smiling. "The new party secretary in the hospital decided your father has completed his re-education. He will be working as a doctor again."

"I would have been home earlier." Father wrapped his arms around us. "But the police wanted to make only one trip. I had to wait until they were ready to arrest Comrade Li and Comrade Sin. Oh, we can't call them Comrade anymore, can we?"

We laughed until our stomachs were sore, echoing the cheers in the courtyard. When I looked up, I saw my hidden hope through Mao's smiling face. I vowed that someday I would find my way to the Golden Gate Bridge.

Author's Note

Although this is a work of fiction, many of the scenes and characters in the book are based on or inspired by real places, actual events, and people from my childhood.

I grew up in the compound of City Hospital Number 4 in Wuhan, where my parents worked. My father graduated from a medical school taught by American missionaries before the Communist Revolution. He was a well-known general surgeon. He taught me English and dancing, and together we listened to the BBC and took trips to a pastry shop.

During the Cultural Revolution, he openly disagreed with Mao and was accused of being an American spy and antirevolutionary. He was forced to work as a janitor in the hospital and later arrested and imprisoned in the city jail after refusing to collaborate with the officials to persecute one of his friends. Through those years, he treated antirevolutionary patients in secret and performed surgery on jail guards and Communist officials. On many occasions, I went to look for him when he was working late at the hospital, treating patients in his janitor's uniform.

After Mao's death, my father became the director of the surgical department and the executive editor of the prestigious *Modern China Surgical Journal*. He came to the United States in 1990 with my mother, but missed his practice and patients and went back to Wuhan a year later. He worked at the hospital until he died on May 9, 1996, surrounded by his family, patients, friends, and colleagues.

My mother was a traditional Chinese medicine doctor. During the Cultural Revolution, she was forced to work the night shift as a nurse in the emergency room because she refused to draw a class line and divorce my father.

I have two brothers. Niu was inspired by one, as well as by a neighbor boy who lived upstairs. My brothers avoided being sent to the countryside for re-education, but were never allowed to attend high school and university. Both were factory workers for many years and still live in Wuhan with their families.

I started this book shortly after my parents passed away. It was then that I realized how much I miss China—the country I love so deeply.

Historical Background

The Communist Party took over China in 1949. The ensuing power struggle among the Communist leaders resulted in Mao Zedong launching the Cultural Revolution in 1966.

Chairman Mao wanted to destroy the culture of pre-Communist China and to regain power from his opponents. With the help of his wife, Jiang Qing, Mao organized the Red Guard, composed of middle school and high school students. Led by Mao's followers from the People's Liberation Army, the Red Guard imprisoned and murdered millions of intellectuals, opposition leaders, and anyone who spoke against Mao's ideology.

Mao's power reached its peak during the middle of the Cultural Revolution. During those years, everyone in China had to carry a little red book and wear Mao-style clothes and buttons bearing his portrait. Radio and loudspeakers broadcasted Mao's quotations and revolutionary songs. Every home and public building and space was decorated with Mao statues and quotations. China's economy reeled. Stores were empty and goods rationed.

Students were encouraged to rebel against teachers and inform on their politically incorrect seniors—including their parents—and act as an ideological militia to ensure the victory of Mao's massive cleansing of his opponents.

While the Cultural Revolution officially ended in 1969 and the worst abuses stopped, the politically charged atmosphere continued until Mao's death on September 9, 1976.

On October 6, less than a month later, the new chairman of the Chinese Communist Party, Hua Guofeng, ordered the arrest of Jiang Qing and her conspirators, the so-called Gang of Four. Jiang Qing was sentenced to death, later changed to life imprisonment. In 1991, she reportedly committed suicide in jail.

Today, China is still a Communist country, but perhaps in name only. Even though the government is a powerful dictatorship, in recent years it has instituted many free-market and capitalist-style reforms to the economy. This has led to joint ventures with foreign companies and an enormous increase in the standard of living for millions of people. Goods are no longer rationed; many are now imported from all over the world. After a long slumber, China is awakening and taking its place on the world stage.

Discussion Questions

1. The title of this book comes from a passage in Chairman Mao's *Little Red Book*:

   "A revolution is not a dinner party, or writing an essay, or painting a picture, or doing embroidery; it cannot be so refined, so leisurely and gentle, so temperate, kind, courteous, restrained, and magnanimous."

   Why do you think the author chose to take the title from this passage?

2. Why do you think Chairman Mao was so easily able to turn neighbors against neighbors during the Cultural Revolution?

3. Ling's mother is able to sense early on that things in China are changing (on page 11, Ling notes that her mother has been in a bad mood for almost a year). What early indications does the author give that "danger [is] knocking on doors all over China"?

4. Why does Ling's mother disapprove of so much of her behavior? Why do you think Mother seems to Ling "like a proud white rose," which Ling is "afraid to touch because of [the] thorns"?

5. A propaganda film is a film produced (often by a government) to convince the viewer of a certain political point or influence the opinions or behavior of people. *Midnight Rooster* in this book is an example of such a film. What effect did watching this film have on the students at Ling's school? Why do you think Ling did not react to the film in the same way as her classmates?

6. What role does food play in the narrative of this book? Why do you think food is so central to the story?

7. Ling's understanding of what bourgeois means changes throughout the book. Based on the events of the novel, what did the word mean during China's Cultural Revolution? Why was it bad for a family to be bourgeois?

8. Father chose to stay in China—rather than go to America with Dr. Smith—to help build a new China. The rally cry of Comrade Li's Red Guard is also for a new China. Why are the two groups (people like Ling's parents and devotees of Chairman Mao) not able to work together to build a new China?

9. When Ling asks Mother why her family needs to hang so many portraits of Mao in their apartment, Mother explains, "It's like the incense we burn in the summer to keep the mosquitoes away." What does she mean?

10. What does the Golden Gate Bridge represent to Ling and her family?

11. Mr. Ji, the antirevolutionary writer Ling and Father save, says "dark clouds have concealed the sun for too long" before he leaves their apartment. What does he mean?

12. What keeps Ling, Mother, and Father from losing hope like Mr. Ji and the baby doctor did?

13. Why does Father operate on Comrade Sin?

14. Can you think of a time in America's history when the political atmosphere was like that during the Cultural Revolution in China? Why do you think people, no matter what country they live in, behave this way?

SQUARE FISH

For more information about Square Fish books, authors, and illustrators visit
www.squarefishbooks.com.

GOFISH

YING CHANG COMPESTINE

What did you want to be when you grew up?
At first an ice cream saleslady, and then a teacher.

When did you realize you wanted to be a writer?
After I lost both of my parents to cancer, I realized how much I missed them and China. I found that writing keeps me close to them.

What's your first childhood memory?
My first taste of imported chocolate, when I was five.

What's your most embarrassing childhood memory?
When talking to a boy I had a crush on, I noticed that my toes stuck out of holes in my worn-out shoes.

What's your favorite childhood memory?
Learning English from my father.

As a young person, who did you look up to most?
Scarlett O'Hara from *Gone with the Wind*. I admired her strength and perseverance.

What was your worst subject in school?
The Revolutionary History of Communist China.

What was your best subject in school?
Literature and writing.

What was your first job?
Working as an interpreter for the Seismological Bureau of the Chinese Government.

How did you celebrate publishing your first book?
I cooked a nice meal and invited friends over for a dinner party.

Where do you write your books?
At home on my computer, by a window overlooking my beautiful garden.

Where do you find inspiration for your writing?
Reading and traveling, cooking and eating.

Which of your characters is most like you?
Ling in *Revolution Is Not a Dinner Party*, and Yun in "Tea Eggs" from *A Banquet for Hungry Ghosts*.

When you finish a book, who reads it first?
My family and two of my best friends.

SQUARE FISH

Are you a morning person or a night owl?
Night person for sure!

What's your idea of the best meal ever?
One I cook for myself after a long trip.

Which do you like better: cats or dogs?
Cats, maybe. Pets were not allowed when I was growing up and I am a little afraid of dogs.

What do you value most in your friends?
Honesty, humor, and a positive attitude.

Where do you go for peace and quiet?
Walking on the trail near my home.

What makes you laugh out loud?
My son's jokes.

What's your favorite song?
"Red River Valley."

Who is your favorite fictional character?
Scarlett O'Hara from *Gone with the Wind*.

What are you most afraid of?
Getting up early.

What time of year do you like best?
Spring.

SQUARE FISH

What's your favorite TV show?
Kitchen Nightmares.

If you were stranded on a desert island, who would you want for company?
My family and my close friends.

If you could travel in time, where would you go?
To ancient Egypt. I would be an Egyptian queen like Cleopatra, but with a happy ending.

What's the best advice you have ever received about writing?
Make every word count. Treat each one as if it was a precious pearl. Don't write a single note, but a symphony.

What do you want readers to remember about your books?
The memorable characters, engaging plot, and surprise ending.

What would you do if you ever stopped writing?
Play badminton at my club every day.

What do you like best about yourself?
How I raised my son.

What is your worst habit?
Checking my e-mail too often.

What do you consider to be your greatest accomplishment?
Writing and publishing *Revolution*. It took me over six years to complete.

Where in the world do you feel most at home?
Wuhan, China.

What do you wish you could do better?
Driving. I am working on overcoming my fear of driving on highways.

What would your readers be most surprised to learn about you?
I have traveled all over the world, including the Antarctic.
    Some weeks I spend over sixteen hours playing badminton at my club with people twenty years younger than me and still manage to beat them.

Hungry ghosts have come back to haunt the living.
But can they be appeased with food?

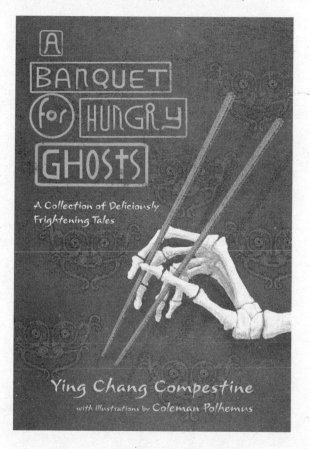

Keep reading for an excerpt from

A Banquet for Hungry Ghosts

available in hardcover from HENRY HOLT.

Steamed Dumplings

LONG AGO, IN 200 B.C.E, there was a small village called Bright Stars situated in the northern mountains of China, along the midsection of the Great Wall. The winter was harsh when this section of the wall was constructed. Heavy snowdrifts blocked the narrow paths through the rugged mountains. For months, supply caravans could not make it through to the workforce.

That winter, some of the workers mysteriously vanished. Everyone was puzzled as to where they had gone: There were no roads out, and with no food, the escapees would surely perish in the cold. Desperate to stop the disappearances, the camp master divided the workers into small teams and issued an order to punish the entire unit if one member deserted.

Despite food shortages, workers were forced to labor day and night in two shifts to meet the emperor's demands—one mile of wall per day. Everyone struggled to survive.

However, one inn—the Double Happy—never seemed to run out of food. It served the best steamed dumplings anyone had ever tasted. No one knew how the owner, Mu, a portly and crafty middle-aged man, got the supplies to make his dumplings so delicious.

After the winter storms cut off the caravans, Mu raised his prices daily. Even so, hungry workers waited in long lines outside his inn. Everyone talked enviously about the fortune he was making.

One cold night after the inn had closed, two starving workers broke into the kitchen. They hoped to steal some food before heading to their evening shift. The taller one, with a rope tied around his bulky cotton jacket, tiptoed in behind his friend, whose ragged fur hat covered most of his face.

Full moonlight shone through the tall windows, leaving streaks of illumination on the kitchen floor. In the far corner, white mist hovered above a huge bamboo steamer on the stove. The scrumptious smell aroused their hunger and made them weak. As they reached for the dumplings, they heard scraping and chopping sounds from behind a cabinet next to the stove. They pushed the cabinet away from the wall, revealing a small door. Fur Hat opened it. Instantly, the pungent odors of garlic, ginger, pickled cabbage, meat, and blood repelled them back a step. Mu, the innkeeper, stood silhouetted in the yellow light of an oil lamp. With a cleaver in each hand he hacked at a dark mound of red meat on a heavy rectangular table. Near him, in a pile on the floor, were arms and legs! Most of them had had the meat stripped from their white bones.

When Mu noticed Fur Hat and Cotton Jacket, he waved his cleavers about wildly and ran toward them. Fur Hat was a trained kung-fu fighter. He pushed his friend aside and swept his left leg across the innkeeper's face, knocking him to the ground. The innkeeper's knives whipped narrowly past Fur Hat. The blood from them drew inky red lines on the wooden floor.

The two workers dragged Mu across the room. Cotton Jacket took the rope from his waist and tied the innkeeper's hands to the table's thick legs.

"You watch over him," Fur Hat said as he ran toward the door. "I'll go report this."

"No!" begged the innkeeper. "Please, I'll make you both wealthy. You will never go hungry again."

Fur Hat stopped, glanced at the flesh on the cutting board, and spat at the innkeeper. "How dare you offer me this disgusting meat! I would rather die of hunger—"

"No, no! Of course not! I have roasted chicken, smoked fish, and rice cakes for you." He jerked his chin toward the dark corner. "There, in those jars."

Cotton Jacket reached into one of the jars and took out a chicken wing. He bit into it. Thick brown sauce ran down his large hand. The innkeeper's face lit up. "Well, how about untying me and we'll talk."

Cotton Jacket stopped stuffing his pockets with preserved duck eggs. "How did you kill them?" He tried hard not to look at the bloody pile as he asked.

"Easy!" A grin emerged upon the innkeeper's face. "Like drunk chickens. Whenever I ran out of meat, I offered my last customers some strong sorghum wine. None of them ever refused, and they drank it like water. Once they passed out, I slit their throats. Most of them didn't even wake."

"You devil!" Cotton Jacket ran over and kicked the innkeeper in his side. The innkeeper moaned sharply.

"We can't be late for our shift," said Fur Hat, as he grabbed pieces of salted fish from a jar. "Let's decide what to do with him in the morning."

Ignoring the innkeeper's pleas, they moved the cabinet back into place, locked the door, and headed out into the cold.

That night, a section of the wall collapsed, burying a team of workers alive. Fur Hat and Cotton Jacket were among them.

The next morning, people were puzzled as to why the Double Happy didn't open. Three days later, a group of hungry workers broke in. They ate everything they could find, including the rock-hard, frozen dumplings in the steamer.

Before long, they noticed many large rats with shiny eyes and wiry whiskers, scurrying out from behind the cabinet.

Each carried a strip of dark red meat. The workers moved the cabinet and found the door. Thinking they'd discovered a secret cache of food, they crowded into the room and then quickly fought to get out, shrieking and vomiting as they ran away.

Inside, the innkeeper's trussed body slumped against the table. Scattered near him were the clothes, shoes, and bones of the missing workers.

Large gray rats ran up and down the innkeeper's body, tearing at the remaining tattered organs. Part of his left cheek was missing—and his face was frozen in a primal scream.

That was the last day anyone ever entered the inn, until many years later . . .